The Sheikh's Assistant

Emily Walters

The Sheikh's Assistant

Published by Emily Walters

Copyright © 2019 by Emily Walters

ISBN 978-1-07045-133-6

First printing, 2019

www.EmilyWaltersBooks.com

PRINTED IN THE UNITED STATES OF AMERICA

Dedication

I want to dedicate this book to my beloved husband, who makes every day in my life worthwhile. Thank you for believing in me when nobody else does, giving me encouragement when I need it the most, and loving me simply for being myself.

Table of Contents

CHAPTER 1 1

CHAPTER 2 8

CHAPTER 3 14

CHAPTER 4 23

CHAPTER 5 31

CHAPTER 6 38

CHAPTER 7 45

CHAPTER 8 55

CHAPTER 9 61

CHAPTER 10 68

CHAPTER 11 74

CHAPTER 12 80

CHAPTER 13 88

CHAPTER 14 93

CHAPTER 15 100

CHAPTER 16 106

CHAPTER 17 113

CHAPTER 18.. 118

EPILOGUE 125

WHAT TO READ NEXT? 128

ABOUT EMILY WALTERS 131

ONE LAST THING... 132

Chapter 1

"It's not ready," Morgan said. Everyone in the conference room turned around to look at her with question marks on their faces. Her friend Brooke leaned closer to her and asked her if she was crazy. Morgan knew that speaking out against the sheikh was a very bold move but it had to be done. She did not think that the drug was ready to be used in clinical trials.

"Who said that?" Sheikh Sofian Bukhari asked. Finely dressed in an expensive charcoal grey suit and black shirt, he was standing at the front of the conference room, His silky jet-black hair was neatly cut short back and sides. His dark eyebrows framed his face, and intensified his dark gaze. His stubble was just a few day old. He had just the right sized lips, not too thin and not too thick. He had a straight nose and strong jaw to complete his perfect face.

"I did," said Morgan.

"What are you doing?" Brooke whispered.

"The drug isn't ready," Morgan whispered back.

"He's the expert and he says that it's ready," Brooke said, referring to the sheikh.

The sheikh walked towards Morgan. His long legs closed the distance pretty quickly. Each stride was filled with so much authority. Everyone stared at him as he approached Morgan.

"Now he's coming here," Brooke whispered. Morgan could tell that she was nervous. She was too. It was their first time being in such close proximity to the sheikh nor had they interacted with him. His family owned Bukhari Pharmaceuticals, and they were royals. Morgan and Brooke were low-level researchers that did not attend the important meetings, and this was their first real meeting. They had been allowed to attend because the sheikh had requested the presence of everyone who had anything to do with research for that drug.

"I know," Morgan whispered back.

"Why isn't it ready?" the sheikh asked her.

"She doesn't know what she's saying. It's definitely ready," said Joe Smith, Morgan's manager. He looked at her sternly, as if he was warning her to keep quiet. Morgan shrugged her shoulders and played with her fingers. She knew that it was not her place to speak out but she felt that she really had to. She did not feel that the drug was ready to enter phase two of the clinical trials.

The sheikh stood in front of Morgan with his arms folded over his chest. He did not pay much attention to what Joe had just said. Morgan swallowed nervously.

"I really do not think it's ready," she said. She felt a little bit intimidated. She was the only one in that entire room that thought so. Everyone else was either not saying anything or urging for the drug to enter the second phase.

"Why do you think it's not ready?" he asked her again.

"The pharmacokinetics suggest that there may be some side effects that would cause hormonal changes in women."

"What?" Joe whipped his head in her direction. He was looking at her like she had very well lost her mind. Brooke raised her eyebrows and looked at Morgan.

"There may be?" Sheikh Bukhari repeated.

"There is," said Morgan.

"There isn't," Joe interrupted.

"How certain are you?" said Sheikh Bukhari.

"Very," said Morgan.

"Everyone can leave, you stay behind."

Brooke and Morgan looked at each other. "Watch what you say," Brooke whispered to Morgan before she stood up and left the room. Morgan had a habit of saying what she thought. She did not beat around the bush and she certainly did not sugarcoat anything.

3

Morgan laced her fingers together as she waited for everyone to leave the conference room. They all looked at her as they left. It seemed that everyone thought she was a fool for speaking out, especially in the sheikh's presence. One wrong word, and Morgan could lose her job. She had heard of the sheikh's short temper and no-nonsense personality. It made her nervous that he had asked her to stay behind and speak to him.

"So, tell me what your views are on this drug," said the sheikh, after the room was empty.

"It needs some adjusting. There is potential to cause side effects," said Morgan as she rose to her feet.

"Hormonal changes, you say."

Morgan nodded. "Yes, sir."

"Which department do you work in?"

"I work in the pharmaceutical lab, north wing."

Sheikh Bukhari raised his eyebrows slightly. "As what?" he asked her.

"Research assistant."

"What are your qualifications?"

Morgan frowned slightly. She was telling him that his drug was not ready, but he was questioning her qualifications and her job position. It was hardly the time. "I have a degree in biomedical science," she said softly and stopped there. She wanted to ask why it was relevant.

"So you do not have much foundation in chemistry?"

Morgan narrowed her gaze. She knew where he was going with this, he did not think she knew what she was talking about. She did not have any qualifications in chemistry, nor did she hold a good position within the company.

"I do not, but I have been working on this drug for almost a year now. I have noted down all of the abnormalities and have analyzed it. I am pretty sure that it is not ready. Something needs to be adjusted, so that there are no effects on female hormones," said Morgan.

"Why should I believe what you are saying?"

"You do not have to, you just have to see for yourself."

"Further testing costs money."

"But it will benefit you in the long run."

"And if you are wrong?"

"I am not wrong."

"You are overconfident," he said with displeasure.

"I am not being overconfident." Morgan fingered a lock of her curly hair. Most of it had been tucked into a high bun, but a lock had managed to fall out. "Sheikh Bukhari, I would not have said anything if I was not sure," she added.

He did not say anything for a moment. He just studied her instead. He slightly tilted his head to the side and just looked at her. Morgan felt a little bit awkward. Not only was he incredibly attractive, he was also her boss who held her job in his hands and he was a cold man. He did not have a friendly or warm presence. His stone-cold gaze sent shivers down her spine.

"Bring me a report first thing tomorrow morning, then I will decide," he said at last.

Morgan nodded. "I will."

Morgan wanted to run out immediately. It was far too awkward and intimidating to be in his presence. She was grateful for her hazelnut-colored skin that did not turn red.

"You may go." He dismissed her with a wave of his hand. Morgan felt that the hand dismissal gesture was rude but she could not say anything about it, not if she wanted to keep her job. She turned on her heel and just left the room.

Morgan felt nervous. She had less than a day to write a report for the sheikh. It was not like she had data analysis lying around. She had to start on it immediately and she had to get everything right.

Otherwise her job would probably come to an end. The sheikh was known for firing incompetent people. After she had dared to speak out in the meeting, she definitely had to be right.

Chapter 2

Morgan frantically checked her laboratory report for the third time. She had to make sure that no mistake could be spotted. After boldly speaking out in front of the sheikh, she had to back up her words.

Brooke walked into the room and stood right in front of Morgan. "I bet you regret it now," Brooke said.

Morgan slightly jumped as she looked up. "You gave me a fright," said Morgan.

Brooke laughed a little. "Now you are scared." Brooke folded her arms over her chest. "This is why you should have just kept quiet like I told you to."

"I do not regret my words. I really do believe that the drug is not ready. Of course I had to say something."

"That is the problem, you always have to say something."

"I do not."

"You know it's true."

"I know." Morgan started laughing. Her mouth had gotten her into trouble so many times. She looked at the laboratory report and ran through the results one more time. They made sense, the proof was right there in black and white. She nodded to herself.

"What time do you have to meet him anyway?" Brooke asked.

"At 9 o'clock," Morgan mumbled.

"Oh, because it's 8:58 right now."

Morgan whipped her head in Brooke's direction. "What?" she spat out. She gathered her paperwork frantically and ran out of the room. The last thing she could afford was tardiness. Morgan rushed out of the laboratory area and headed to the elevator. She pressed the call button.

"Come on," she whispered as she waited impatiently. She pressed the elevator button a couple of times more.

It finally arrived seconds later. To Morgan, it had felt like hours. She quickly walked in when the doors opened. She pressed the button for the 12th floor. She cursed under her breath when she realized that she only knew the floor number but not the exact location of his office. Why would she know it? After all she had never been there.

As soon as the doors opened, Morgan rushed out. Like a chicken with its head cut off, she ran around the place looking for his office. Her eyes widened when she saw a man dressed in a suit. He looked important enough to know the sheikh. She rushed over to him. "Excuse me, do you know where Sheikh Bukhari's office is?" she asked him.

"His office is down the hall, to the right. It's the one at the end of the corridor," he said to her with a smile. Morgan barely waited for him to finish speaking, before she ran off.

"Thank you," she said as she ran.

Morgan reached the sheikh's office seconds later. There was a small reception area outside his office. A neatly dressed woman sat at the reception desk. She looked up as Morgan arrived.

"I have an appointment with the sheikh," Morgan said to her.

"Yes, he is expecting you," the woman replied as she rose from her seat. She went and knocked at the office door before she entered. Morgan heard her tell the sheikh that she was there. "You may go in," the woman said to Morgan.

The sheikh was standing by the window with his hands in his pockets when Morgan walked in. He had his back towards the door. Morgan could not help but notice how broad his back was. His black shirt complemented his strong and wide back.

"You are late," said Sheikh Sofian Bukhari. Morgan almost jumped when he spoke. She had been too fixated on his back.

"Ah, yeah, er, I was lost," she replied. She could not even find the proper words to say.

Sofian turned around and looked at her. "That is not a plausible excuse."

Morgan glanced at the glass clock hung on his wall. It was 9:04. She was only four minutes late. It seemed that he was as strict as people made him out to be.

"It is not an excuse, it is—"

Before Morgan could finish her sentence, Sofian cut her off. "I am not interested in excuses. Give me the report."

Morgan did not appreciate his rudeness but she had no choice. He was the employer and she was the employee. It did not give him the right to be rude to her but it meant that she was unable to talk back, at least not as much as she wanted. She decided to bite her tongue and just hand him the report she had written.

Sofian took the sheets of paper and looked at them. Morgan felt awkward. She was not sure if she was meant to leave him with the report or if she was meant to stand there and wait for him to finish reading it. He had not specified anything. So Morgan just laced her fingers together and waited for him to tell her what to do.

"The report has an untidy presentation but I see your point," Sofian said after a couple of minutes.

Morgan raised her recently threaded eyebrows. "Untidy?" she mumbled.

"Yes. This paragraph is not aligned properly," he pointed out.

Morgan narrowed her gaze. "But do you see what I mentioned about the new medicine?" she asked. That was the point of the document, and not alignment of the paragraphs.

Sofian looked at her with a blank facial expression. "I prefer everything to be done neatly."

"Very well," said Morgan.

Sofian put the report on his desk. "I do see why you were brazen," he said.

Morgan raised her eyebrows again. "I was brazen?" she asked him.

"Yes. It takes guts for a person in your position to speak out on something important, and against everyone else's professional opinions."

"Exactly, everyone has a professional opinion and I was giving mine."

"And I am saying that it was a brass move."

"Maybe, but it was necessary."

Sofian did not say anything for a moment. He just looked at Morgan. It made her feel uneasy. She had no clue as to what he was thinking. Nevertheless, she was not going to allow him to intimidate her. She squared her shoulders and stared him down.

"Before the meeting, had you seen me before? Have we met?" Sofian asked her.

"No," Morgan replied. "Why?"

"Nothing. You may go."

Not that Morgan expected some kind of reward or anything, but he should at least have thanked her for spotting such an important side effect. Had she not brought the issue up at the meeting, the drug may have entered the next phase. The sheikh only read the report and then just dismissed her. He had not even praised her or thanked her. Nothing!

"Okay." Morgan turned on her heel and left his office. After having asked her if they had met before, Sofian offered no explanation and then just dismissed her.

Chapter 3

Sofian called for a meeting instantly. He needed to sit down with the other managers and discuss where to go from there. Even though he had not admitted it to Morgan, he was impressed by her. She had spotted something very important and spoke out.

He was incredibly surprised at how bold she was. She had never met him before, and she held such a low position within the company. And yet she was not afraid of him, like most people were. All the other employees did not dare to speak their minds in his presence, and in some cases did not even look him in the eye.

Sofian got up from his desk and headed to the conference room, where the meeting was to be held. He was meeting with all the managers that had anything to do with this new drug. Now that there was proof of what Morgan had suggested at the meeting, the drug needed further testing. They needed to make it safer.

When Sofian entered the conference room, the managers all rose to their feet and bowed their heads. Sofian walked in with so much authority in his stride. He went to sit at the head of the long mahogany table. The managers waited for him to sit down before they too sat down. Sofian had Morgan's laboratory report in his hand. He placed it on the table and then leaned back into his leather chair.

"This is a report done by a low-level researcher," said Sofian. "She was able to find something that none of you were able to."

The managers looked at each other. "Sheikh, what do you mean?" one of them asked.

"Take a look for yourself," Sofian replied. The manager sitting to his right reached out for the report and started reading it.

Sofian looked at Joe Smith. "I remember you at the meeting trying to shut that girl up."

"Sheikh, it was not her place to speak," said Joe.

"And yet she was correct to do so."

"Sheikh?"

"She was the only person that noticed that the medicine would have such side effects. Look at the report for yourself."

Joe took the report from the other manager and looked at it. His eyes flew open when he started reading it. He looked at the results and the graphs that Morgan had prepared. "Impossible," he mumbled.

"This is so disappointing," said Sofian. "I wonder if you are at all worthy of your jobs."

Sofian did not tolerate mistakes. He was a perfectionist and was quite strict with his staff. He was in the pharmaceutical industry. This involved making medicine. No mistakes could be made. Sofian was not happy with the fact that no one had noticed the side effects except for Morgan, a low-level researcher.

"Please forgive us for not noticing the side effects," said Paul Davis, one of the other managers. Sofian looked at him.

"Did you not think to retest the drug?" Sofian asked him.

"We conducted different tests on it."

"Clearly not enough was done. Otherwise we would not be having this discussion right now." Sofian slightly raised his voice. He was getting even more annoyed with the fact that they were giving excuses. He hated excuses so much.

"Please do not be upset with us. We will do more testing," said one of the other managers.

"What annoys me even more, is the fact that when Morgan spoke up, none of you even considered the possibility. Instead you ignored her and tried to shut her up."

"We were wrong," said Joe.

"Of course you were wrong. A low-level researcher does a better job than all of you."

"Please—"

Before Joe finished speaking, Sofian dismissed him with his hand. "I should fire you really but we will just move forward. More testing needs to be done. This drug has to be safe for pregnant women. It must not harm the woman or the baby," said Sofian. The new drug they were creating was to help women with morning sickness.

"Yes, sir," said Paul.

"You must eradicate all side effects. I will not tolerate any mistakes this time around," Sofian warned.

"Yes, sheikh," the managers chorused. Sofian shook his head as he stood up. The managers also stood up.

"Thank you for your mercy," said Paul. Sofian offered no response. He just walked out of the room. All he needed from that point was results. He did not want any more mistakes, nor did he want any excuses.

***

Days had passed since Morgan had given the sheikh the laboratory report. Joe Smith was not particularly pleased with Morgan. He felt that she had embarrassed him in front of the sheikh. He felt that she should have passed the results to him first.

Morgan was annoyed because she actually did try to approach him about it initially, but he shut her down.

"I can't believe Joe is still giving you grief about all of this," said Brooke as they sat down for lunch in the company cafeteria.

"Tell me about it," Morgan replied. She shook her head before she bit into her burger. Her mother had been asking her to eat better. She knew that she had to cut back on the junk foods but she loved eating too much.

"I can't believe that sheikh did not even give you a reward or anything."

Morgan laughed before she responded. "I guess keeping my job is a good reward," she replied.

"Why would he fire you?"

"That man is unpredictable." Morgan sighed. She had only spoken to him on two different occasions but it was enough to form an opinion of him. He was simply an arrogant, cold man. He definitely was not friendly or humble.

"Excuse me, Morgan?" a voice sounded. Both Morgan and Brooke turned towards the voice. Morgan recognized the person instantly, it was the sheikh's assistant.

"Hi," Morgan greeted her with food in her mouth. Brooke frowned at her for being so unladylike.

"The sheikh wants to see you."

"Me? Why?"

"I do not know but he asks that you come at once."

"Okay." Morgan stood up. "I'll see you later," she said to Brooke and then followed Sofian's assistant back to his office. Morgan still had her burger in her hand as they walked. She made sure to finish it before they reached the sheikh's office.

The sheikh was leaning on his desk when Morgan arrived. "You asked to see me?" she said awkwardly as she walked in.

He did not respond straight away. Instead he just looked at her.

"I did," he finally said. "Come here."

Morgan did as told. He handed her a folder. "What is it?" she asked him.

"Look at it," he ordered. Morgan opened the folder. There was a list of ingredients for a child-friendly painkiller. She looked at the sheikh quizzically. She did not understand why he was giving her that information.

"New medicine?" she asked.

Sofian nodded. "What are your thoughts on the ingredients?"

"I am confused," said Morgan. It did not make sense to her why he would ask for her thoughts on ingredients.

"I want a child-friendly painkiller, and these are the ingredients I want to include."

Morgan looked at the list again. "Well, if you are aiming for children, I think you should use less chemicals. The more natural the better. Also something flavored would be good," she said. She put the list back in the folder and handed it back to him.

Sofian kept a blank expression. He gave nothing away. "I think you are wrong. This list is just fine," he said.

Morgan raised her eyebrows. "Sheikh Bukhari, most of those chemicals and herbs do not go well together," she said in the most respectful tone she could muster. It surprised her that a man of his talents would make such a simple error.

"Are you sure about that?"

"I am." Morgan nodded. Sofian threw the folder in the small office waste bin by his desk. Morgan frowned. She was even more confused.

"Starting from tomorrow you will no longer be a researcher."

"What?" Morgan spat out.

"You will be working up here as my assistant instead."

"What?"

"I do not like to repeat myself."

"I am confused," Morgan said. Sofian narrowed his gaze at her. "Am I being promoted?"

"You cannot be this slow," said Sofian.

"Well, you are not being particularly clear."

Sofian sighed with frustration. "Morgan, I want you to work as my personal assistant, for more compensation, of course."

"But you already have an assistant."

"She can work on something else. Report here at 9 a.m. sharp tomorrow. Do not be late. I know you have a tendency for tardiness."

"I was late just once." Was he still going on about it? Morgan asked herself.

"You may leave."

"Thank you." Morgan turned on her heel to leave. She stopped at the door and looked at Sofian. "You were testing me," she said to him.

"What?"

"That bogus list you gave me. You were testing me."

Sofian shrugged his shoulders in response. It made sense that he was testing her. She had thought that it was strange for him to make such an error. Morgan just opened the door and left his office. She wondered if she had failed his test, whether he would still have promoted her.

Chapter 4

Sofian sat in his office reading over some paperwork. He looked at the gold Rolex sitting on his wrist. There were only five minutes left till 9 o'clock. It would be a shame if Morgan arrived late on her first day working for him. He had hired her to replace his current assistant because he could see a lot of potential in Morgan. She was smart. He was impressed by her laboratory findings in regards to the drug.

Morgan was also not afraid to point out what she thought. She had not been afraid to speak up in the conference meeting. And he had shown her that fake list. She was quick to spot the errors and speak out about it. He told her that the list was correct, and she was not afraid to disagree with him. He needed a candid assistant. He did not want a "yes sir, no sir" type of assistant.

"Good morning, Sheikh Bukhari," Morgan said as she walked into his office. Sofian looked at the time. There was only a minute left.

"You are on time," Sofian said to Morgan.

"I am."

He could not help but study her outfit. Anyone working closely with him needed to be dressed well.

She was not dressed badly. She wore a high-waisted blue skirt and a white blouse. Her clothes showed off her hourglass figure. Her curly hair was neatly tucked into a high bun. She wore small studs.

Sofian rose from his desk and approached Morgan. She was so much shorter than he was, especially since she was in flats. Her head reached his chest. "Come with me," he said to her.

"Okay." Morgan nodded her head. She followed him out of the office. They stopped at the reception area outside his office.

"This will be your work space," he told her.

"What happened to your assistant?"

"What does that have to do with you?"

"I am just curious if I am taking her job or not."

Sofian raised his eyebrows. Usually a person would be happy to be promoted. He could not understand why Morgan was so curious about it. She had mentioned it the day before.

"I have moved her to a different department," he said. Morgan stared at him blankly. "You do not believe me."

"I never said that." Morgan shifted awkwardly.

"But you thought it."

"No, I did not."

"Well, she is working in the sales department, if you wish to look for her." Sofian did not understand why he was even explaining himself. He was never one to do so. Morgan opened her mouth to speak but Sofian raised his hand to stop her. "You will be responsible for my schedule," he began. He told her what her duties were going to be. He already had some work for her that he needed her to get through.

"Okay," Morgan said. Her tone suggested doubt.

"Are you not confident that you can meet my expectations?" he asked her.

"No, Sheikh. I can definitely meet them."

"Good."

Sofian returned to his office. Morgan was left standing by the reception area. She was shocked at how fussy the sheikh was. He wanted everything done right and on time, which was fine but he was specific about the things he wanted. He had explained how she was to organize any reports given to him. The alignment was to be perfect. He even explained what he liked to eat and what he did not want to eat. She was to be responsible for getting his lunch also.

Morgan was not quite sure about the promotion anymore. She liked working in the lab. Now she was to do paperwork and be a waitress for the sheikh. She sighed as she walked behind the desk. She started moving things around and just reorganizing. She needed it to be more her style.

"What are you doing?" Morgan heard Sofian's voice. He caught her off guard, she almost jumped out of her skin. She turned to face him. She found him leaning in the doorway of his office, looking at her.

"Oh, you scared me," she mumbled.

"Why do you look like you were caught stealing?" He looked amused.

"I am just fixing the desk."

"Because?"

"Just so I know where everything is." Morgan looked around. "Now it feels more like my style."

Sofian raised an eyebrow. "Okay, then."

"Was there anything that I could do for you, sir?" Morgan asked.

"Yes, some green tea."

"How would you like it?"

"Green."

A small smile appeared on Morgan's face. She did not understand whether Sofian was joking or being serious. He had said something sarcastic but he barely changed his facial expression. He did not laugh or anything.

"Oh, okay, because I was going to make it purple. Do you take sugar or honey?" Morgan could not help but return the sarcasm. She could almost hear Brooke telling her that it was a bad move. Brooke often told Morgan to cut back on her sarcasm and perhaps bite her tongue in most situations. Morgan knew that this was the time she should have taken Brooke's advice. She barely knew the sheikh to be sarcastic towards him. Besides he was her boss. He had her job in his hands. She had to be careful.

"Neither. Just make it strong," said Sofian. He turned on his heel and returned to his office. Morgan felt relieved that he did not comment on her sarcasm. She rushed off to the kitchen to make the tea.

When lunchtime arrived, Morgan welcomed it eagerly. She had spent the morning photocopying documents, making phone calls and organizing the sheikh's schedule for the week. She brought the sheikh his food before she went to meet with Brooke for lunch.

"Here she comes," Brooke said as Morgan approached her. She seemed so excited to see Morgan.

"Hey," Morgan said with no emotion.

"How is it so far?"

"Boring."

"What? You are working for the sheikh, a prince of Kaslan! How could that be boring?"

"I am doing a lot of paperwork. That stuff is boring. I miss working in the lab with you guys." Morgan pouted.

Brooke raised an eyebrow. "If I was in your position, I would not be thinking of the lab or anyone in it."

Morgan narrowed her gaze at Brooke. "It's really not that great working for him, you know," she said before she bit into her sandwich.

"Why not?"

"He's so fussy, and there are these weird moments when he is looking at me and not saying anything. It's so scary because I do not know what he is thinking. I am always on edge."

Brooke threw her head backwards and started laughing. "Morgan, you are so dramatic," she said and started laughing again.

"What?"

"You have only been working for him for like four hours."

"So?"

"How are you always on edge?"

"Well in those four hours I was on edge." Morgan laughed a little. She too knew that she was being so dramatic about it. However she could not help how the sheikh had made her feel.

"Most people are dying to be in your position."

"I have to admit that I was curious about him before I met him. Now that I have, I see that he is an arrogant man. Of course he would be, he is a prince."

"Exactly."

"Also he is unpredictable. He made a sarcastic comment earlier but didn't laugh or anything. It was weird."

"So he's like you?"

"What?" Morgan almost spat out her drink.

"You are both sarcastic and weird." Brooke grinned. Morgan frowned.

"I am not weird," Morgan protested. Brooke just looked at her. "Okay, maybe a little." Morgan burst into laughter.

"Does he smell nice?" Brooke asked her.

"Now that is weird!"

"I am just curious about him, just like any normal woman would be."

"It's not like I was sniffing him."

"Well, do so next time." Brooke giggled a little. Morgan laughed with her. She knew that Brooke liked men that smelled nice. It was one of the things that turned her on. So naturally she would be curious about it. The two of them continued having lunch together and talking about all sorts of things.

Chapter 5

The next day, Morgan was sitting at her desk when the sheikh arrived. He was dressed in a black pair of trousers and a navy-blue shirt. Such a simple outfit complemented his muscular physique and highlighted his impressive height. Morgan rose from her desk to greet him as he approached.

"Good morning, Sheikh. I'll get your tea," said Morgan.

"You're early," Sofian said to her. Morgan refrained from frowning at him. She was right on time and only early by a minute but he did not seem to be letting it go.

"I am," she replied with fake enthusiasm. Sofian did not offer a response. He just walked into his office. Morgan rushed to the kitchen to get his green tea ready. While she was waiting for the water to boil, his former assistant walked into the kitchen. Morgan immediately smiled at her.

"Hello," Morgan greeted her.

"How is my job?" Sofian's former assistant asked. Morgan's face dropped. That was not the response she was expecting.

"Pardon?"

"You did steal my job and I am just asking if you are enjoying it."

"I, stole, your job?" Morgan could not believe what she was hearing. Sofian's former assistant should have known that the sheikh was more than capable of replacing her whenever he pleased. It was not like Morgan went out of her way to get that job. It just happened that way.

"You know you wanted it."

"The sheikh just offered it to me."

"Well, you accepted."

"So you wanted me to refuse it?"

"Working for the sheikh is not as easy as you think it is. You will soon learn it." The sheikh's former assistant eyeballed Morgan from head to toe. "You won't last longer than two months. I've worked for him for two years, so I know that you do not have what it takes. I've always come back to my position." With that she left the kitchen.

Morgan sighed. The jealousy that was oozing out of Sofian's former assistant was disturbing. Morgan had not asked for that position. At first she was not so keen on it but after that threat, she was definitely going to do everything she could to keep it. She was not going to give that woman the satisfaction. Morgan had to last longer than two months. She quickly prepared the sheikh's tea and then headed back to his office.

"Here is your tea," Morgan said to Sofian as she placed it on the table. Sofian took the cup and sipped his tea. He looked up.

"Was there something else?" he asked Morgan who was standing there.

"No. Yes."

"What is it?"

"Your former assistant, was she with you for two years?"

Sofian narrowed his gaze at her. "Why must you bring her up again?" he asked her. Morgan shifted awkwardly.

"I met her in the kitchen."

"So?"

"She told me that she had worked for you for two years."

"And?"

"She mentioned that she always came back to her position. Have you let her go before?"

Sofian shrugged his shoulders. "And if I have?" he asked.

"It's just that if she was with you for that long, wouldn't you consider keeping her on?" Morgan asked. It all did not make sense to her. If his assistant was doing a bad job, then he would not have kept her for that long. However if she was doing a good job then why did he hire Morgan to replace her?

"I change my assistants whenever I feel the need to," said Sofian. It did not really answer her question but she knew she had to stop there. She couldn't keep asking questions.

"Okay, I understand that." Morgan smiled and left the office. She returned to her desk to get some work done. Later that day she and Sofian were going for a meeting together. He had to meet with the board members of Jackie's Pharmacies. It was a chain of pharmacies all over the United States. Sofian needed to finalize a deal with them so that they could sell Bukhari Pharmaceuticals products.

It was going to be Morgan's first meeting as Sofian's assistant. She had never attended such an important meeting before. She had gone from being just an ordinary research assistant to being the sheikh's personal assistant; attending important meetings and speaking to people she would have never spoken to. She was a little nervous about it.

When the time came for Sofian and Morgan to leave for the meeting, she did not even need to go look for him. He was out of his office early.

"Shall we go?" he said to her. Morgan rose from her desk and nodded.

"Yes, sir," she replied. She followed him out of the building.

Fortunately, Morgan had already called for the car in case Sofian surprised her by leaving for the meeting early. It would have not been a good sign if he had come out and the car wasn't ready. When they got outside, the chauffeur opened the car door for the sheikh. He looked at Morgan. "After you," he said to her.

Morgan had not expected that at all. "Thank you," she told him. She got into the car. It was quite roomy and comfortable inside. She had never been inside a Rolls-Royce. The cream leather seats were nice and comfortable. Sofian shut the door behind her and got into the car from the other side.

It was a quiet ride to Jackie's Pharmacies headquarters. There was nothing to say between the two of them. Morgan felt extremely awkward because she was not a silent person. However Sofian seemed to be. Conversations between them never went on for longer than five minutes. In some cases, he did not even answer her. He would just look at her with a blank facial expression which drove Morgan crazy.

The car came to a halt. Morgan looked out of the window and realized that they had arrived. "Are you ready?" Sofian asked her.

"Yes, I am." Morgan turned to face him.

"I expect you to be professional and polite."

"Yes, of course."

"Before we go in, do you have any questions?"

"Not really."

"Okay. Make sure you listen well and take notes."

Morgan nodded. "Yes, sir," she said. Sofian nodded and then got out of the car. Morgan also got out of the car. She walked next to Sofian. He even opened the door for her. He was an arrogant man, but at least he was a gentleman.

The board members all greeted the sheikh. As Sofian had asked, Morgan paid attention throughout the meeting. She noticed how they were all so respectful towards Sofian. They were so impressed by him. Morgan was not too surprised. Sofian had so much authority and he was intimidating. He was also a prince, so naturally they would listen to him.

Morgan was surprised about how intelligent and well-spoken he was in the meeting. There was not a hint of the arrogance that he had displayed to her. He was still candid but he was professional. Morgan was impressed and a little turned on. She liked seeing how in control he was, just so dominant and eloquent.

Chapter 6

"Good morning," Morgan greeted Sofian the next morning. She gave him his green tea.

"Morgan," he said.

"Sheikh." Morgan grinned.

"You are peculiar." Sofian took a sip of his tea.

Morgan put her hands out to him as if she was asking for something and gasped. She really did not understand Sofian. He was randomly calling her peculiar. "Why would you say that? What did I do that was peculiar?"

Sofian looked amused. He just took another sip of his green tea. "I need you to contact my lawyer," he said, changing the subject. Morgan still needed an answer as to why he called her peculiar but it was obvious that she was not going to get one. But why did he want her to get his lawyer?

"Did you commit some kind of crime? Do I need to hide a body?"

"What?"

Morgan giggled a little. "Why do you need a lawyer?" she asked him.

He raised his eyebrows slightly. "Peculiar."

"It was a joke," Morgan mumbled. She was starting to regret the joke. Again this was where she could have used Brooke's advice. Some things did not need to be said.

"No, I did not kill anyone or commit any other crime. I need my lawyer to draw up the contract between Bukhari Pharmaceuticals and Jackie's Pharmacies."

"Oh right, okay. I will do that," said Morgan.

"When you are done with that, get these documents photocopied and then filed in order by date."

Morgan picked up the documents from his desk. "Yes, sir," she said.

"Tara was more normal than you," said Sofian. Morgan crossed her eyebrows.

"Who is Tara?" she asked. "Oh, your assistant. That's her name?"

"I am surprised you do not already know that."

"Why?"

"Because you seem so interested in her."

Morgan laughed sarcastically. "It isn't like that at all. She thinks, never mind," she said. She held onto the documents tighter. "I'll go sort these out."

"What does she think?" Sofian asked. Clearly he was curious about what Morgan was about to say.

"That I stole her job."

"Well, she should know better than to think that."

"I am sure anyone would feel that way," said Morgan. That was the only thing she could say. "I'll go deal with these," she said and walked out of the office.

Morgan called Sofian's business lawyer and gave him Sofian's instructions. When she was done speaking to him on the phone, she started with the photocopying. Then the filing. When she was done with that, she started typing other documents. Working for the sheikh was hard work. There were so many different things to do.

The phone buzzed. Morgan answered it. It was Sofian calling her into his office. She rose from her desk and rushed into his office. "How can I assist you?" she asked.

"I need you to pick up my dry cleaning."

Morgan narrowed her gaze. She was not particularly keen about doing that. She had much more work to do, and frankly she missed being in the lab.

"Yes, sir," Morgan replied.

"My driver will take you." Sofian barely looked up from his desk. He was quite busy with his own work.

"Yes, sir." Morgan left his office to go collect his dry cleaning.

Sofian's chauffeur was waiting for Morgan outside the car. He opened the door for her. She smiled and thanked him as she got into the car. It was crazy to her that she was sitting in a car more expensive than everything she owned put together.

The leather seats were so comfortable. There was even an option to recline the seat. And there was also a mini bar and a mini television. She was so impressed by the interior. She was a little surprised too that the sheikh had allowed her to use such an expensive car.

***

Morgan was a little nervous about their meeting the following week. Sofian wanted progress reports on how the morning sickness drug research was going. So he had Morgan send out emails to everyone involved asking them to attend the meeting. Now that the meeting was about to start, Morgan felt nervous about it. Only because of the jealousy that was going around.

Brooke had informed Morgan about the talk that was going around the lab. A handful of people were happy for her and the rest were not. They talked about how she was lucky and did not deserve to be the sheikh's assistant. The managers were particularly annoyed because they felt that she had made them look bad in front of the sheikh. Morgan had also been informed by Brooke that she had been spotted getting into the sheikh's Rolls-Royce. That instantly struck up rumors and jealousy. Morgan could not believe the pettiness.

Sofian and Morgan walked into the conference room after everyone had already sat down. It was a bit odd for Morgan to be walking next to the sheikh. It was a little empowering. She could not help but borrow a little authority from him. At the same time it made Morgan a bit nervous. All eyes were on them. She could hear a few whispers, and she could feel the eyes burning through her.

Sofian sat at the head of the table of course. Morgan sat to his right. She was in full view of everyone. All the managers were sitting around the oval mahogany table. The other researchers and team leaders were sitting on chairs along the wall.

"So what is the progress?" Sofian asked, getting straight to the point. The managers looked at each other, wondering who was to speak first. "Anyone speak, now."

"Ah yes, sir," said Paul. He cleared his throat. "We are still looking at different ways to reduce the side effects."

"So there is no progress?"

The managers looked at each other awkwardly. No one dared to say the words. Sofian sighed heavily. "After all this time, you still have nothing?" Sofian asked them.

"We have been doing experiments, sheikh. We will find a solution soon," said another manager.

"Soon?" Sofian asked. He was clearly not impressed. It was obvious that he was trying to keep from getting angry. Morgan was happy that she was not on the receiving end of his wrath. "Does anyone at least have any ideas of how to improve this medicine?"

There was silence for a moment. No one spoke. Then Paul suggested adding different compounds. Sofian shook his head and shut the idea down. He wanted the medicine to contain very minimal chemical substances. Since the drug was for pregnant women, he did not want the medicine to harm the mother or the baby.

"What about reducing the concentration of the active ingredient?" said Morgan.

Sofian looked at her. "Elaborate," he said to her. Everyone else also looked at her.

"I'm thinking, since you want the medicine to have less chemicals, why don't we reduce the concentration of the chemicals and add more B6 instead?"

"That makes no sense. Why add more B6?" Joe asked.

"B6 has been a key ingredient in relieving nausea in pregnant women," Morgan replied.

"Try Morgan's idea," said Sofian.

"But–"

Before Joe could finish speaking, Sofian cut him off. "Do you have a better idea?"

"No, sir."

"Then do what she said." Sofian got up from his chair and headed out. Everyone else also stood up immediately. Some bowed their heads to him as he walked past. Morgan awkwardly followed him. She quickly waved to Brooke as she left.

Chapter 7

"Interesting idea," Sofian said to Morgan as they walked from the conference room.

"Hmm. It was so interesting that it has gained me some enemies," Morgan mumbled.

Sofian turned his head slightly in Morgan's direction. "Enemies?" he questioned.

"Uh-huh."

"Why?"

"Nothing."

They reached the elevator. Sofian pressed the button and then turned fully to face Morgan. He slid his hands in his pockets. "You spoke up in two different meetings and gained my attention. I promoted you and now people are jealous," he said to her.

Morgan looked up at him. "Yeah, exactly," she replied. Being that close to Sofian was uncomfortable. She was able to really see how magnificent his body was. His muscles were tormenting her. They were calling for her to touch him. She caught a whiff of his scent. He smelled nice. Really nice. Sofian was also looking at her, which made her even more uncomfortable. His jaw twitched.

Fortunately the elevator doors opened.

Morgan cleared her throat and walked into the elevator first. She stood on the left side and clasped her hands together. Sofian walked in after her and stood next to her. The doors shut and they were on their way up.

"So why let jealousy bother you?" he asked her.

"It does not necessarily bother me. I mean these things happen, but it's just ridiculous," she replied.

"It is."

"I mean I am even getting backlash for using your car."

"Maybe because I never let anyone use it."

Morgan whipped her head in his direction. "And you let me use it?" Morgan was shocked.

"It's just a car," Sofian replied. The elevator doors opened and he walked out. Morgan followed behind.

"A seventy thousand dollar car," Morgan pointed out. Sofian barely reacted. He was acting like it was no big deal.

"Yes," he replied.

So Tara never used Sofian's car, like to go somewhere by herself without him in it, Morgan thought to herself. It was an interesting thought. It made her wonder what made her so special to be allowed to use it. Tara must have been getting even more jealous.

"Look." Sofian stopped walking when they reached Morgan's desk. "You are capable of doing a good job. That is why I hired you. If you are having doubts or you are scared of what people think, then quit," he added.

"No, sir. I am not scared nor do I have doubts about my abilities. I know I can execute my role well," she said.

A small smile appeared on his face. "Confident?" he asked.

"Yes."

"Keep it that way." Sofian winked at her and then went into his office. Once again he had shocked Morgan. He had given her half a compliment about how she was capable of doing a good job. Then he gave her half a smile, which was far much more than usual. Then he winked at her. He was really hard to understand. Morgan just sighed and sat at her desk.

***

Sofian was at his desk working when Morgan marched in with a straight face. She was dressed in grey leggings and a white T-shirt with grey sleeves. "You're here," he said to her.

"It's a Saturday," Morgan pointed out. Sofian looked up. From her tone, he could tell that she was not pleased about working during the weekend.

"From time to time, I will require you to work for me during weekends and some late nights. Is that going to be a problem?" Sofian leaned back in his seat and just stared at her.

Morgan placed her hands on her hips. "I would have liked to have known in advance," she mumbled.

"Come here."

Morgan dragged her feet as she approached Sofian's wide glass desk. He gestured for her to sit down. She pulled out one of the two white leather chairs and sat down in front of him. He passed her some documents.

"What are these?" she asked him.

"I need you to help me get through some documents."

Morgan nodded and picked up one of the documents. "What are they for?"

"That child-friendly painkiller, it's real. I need to start that project soon."

Morgan raised her eyebrows. "You have other trials for other medications going on, and not to mention the morning sickness medication research going on. Now this? It's a lot of work. Can you handle it all?"

"Can I handle it? Woman, I am Sofian Bukhari. I can handle anything."

Morgan started laughing. "I will pretend that that did not sound conceited," she said.

He noticed how odd her laugh was. It was not cute or ladylike, but she looked pretty and playful when she laughed. "It's just the truth. The men in my family are built to handle anything," he said.

Morgan smiled and nodded. "Do you have siblings?"

"An older brother. Why do you not know that?"

"Believe it or not, I don't Google you in my spare time."

Sofian smiled. "You should. I have an impressive profile."

Morgan crossed her eyebrows. "Okay, about this painkiller." She looked down at the documents.

"That drug for morning sickness, it needs a name," he said suddenly.

"Um, okay. What a change in topic."

"Name it."

"Name what?"

"I need you to come up with a name for the morning sickness medicine. And this one actually." It was the first time Sofian was ever allowing an assistant to do that. Usually he and the board members came up with any names.

"What? You want me to do that?" she asked. Sofian just looked at her and did not respond. She put the documents down and started thinking. "Nausi Free," she said with a grin on her face.

"Nausi Free? That is a strange name."

"No, it makes sense. Nausi Free, meaning nausea free. It's simple and catchy." Morgan giggled.

"We'll use that then."

"Really?"

"Yes."

"Cool." Morgan tucked a curly lock of hair behind her ear. Sofian noticed that small things excited her. She seemed particularly happy about Nausi-Free. He smiled to himself and returned his attention back to his work.

Sofian was hands-on. He wanted to prepare a rough list of what he wanted in the painkiller drug before he passed it to the relevant team to start the research. He also wanted to set the budget, plan the time scale, choose companies to pitch sales to, and pick out the team he wanted to work on it. He was very hands-on.

A bit later on in the day, Morgan was no longer working. She was sitting there with her jaw in her palm. Sofian noticed. She looked bored.

"What is the matter?" he asked her.

"I am hungry."

"Oh." Sofian narrowed his gaze at her. "I thought that there was actually something wrong with the work, or you."

Morgan looked at him and pouted slightly. "I can't think straight when I am hungry."

Sofian could not help but laugh. Morgan's eyes flew open.

"That is ludicrous," he said.

"Wow, you actually laughed."

"I laugh."

"No, you do not. You don't smile either."

"I find that hard to believe," Sofian replied with an expressionless face.

"You always look so serious."

Sofian pulled out his cell phone. He dialed a number and ordered food. He seemed to know the person but not the menu. He was rather asking that things be prepared a certain way. Morgan watched him with a quizzical look on her face. "What?" he asked her.

"Was that the first time you ever ordered food for yourself?" she asked.

"Yes." Sofian grinned, face full of guilt. He lived a pampered life.

"You know the people?"

"Yes. A friend of mine owns an excellent restaurant down the street. He can get the food prepared and sent over on my call."

"Nice." Morgan smiled and nodded.

"I hope you like lamb," Sofian said to her when the food arrived.

"I like anything edible." Morgan's face lit up. Sofian smiled to himself and said nothing. The two of them moved to the sitting area, away from the paperwork so that they could eat. Sofian could not help but watch Morgan eating. It was the first time he witnessed her eating.

"You are enjoying that," Sofian commented.

"I am," Morgan replied with her mouth full. Sofian raised an eyebrow. It was such an unladylike thing to do. She was not ladylike. She was not like other women. It was refreshing to see a woman actually eat as much as she wanted and enjoy her food.

Morgan was also intelligent. He knew that he had made the right decision to hire her as his assistant. She was full of bright ideas and she amused him at times. He wondered why she was not affected by him. Most women would be affected by him somehow, whether it was intimidation or in most cases attraction. He affected women, everyone in fact. However with Morgan, he could not tell. He was intrigued.

"What are you thinking?" Morgan asked him as she helped herself to more food.

"You are not full?" Sofian asked her.

Morgan narrowed her gaze at him. "Don't judge my appetite."

Sofian smiled. "I am not judging."

"That's the second time you smiled today, wow," Morgan pointed out again.

"I do smile," Sofian said matter-of-factly. Morgan looked doubtful. She did not believe him. "I smile when it is necessary."

Morgan laughed a little. "Okay then," she said. Neither of them spoke after that. They just looked at each other. Sofian took in her looks. She was beautiful. She had these mischievous big brown eyes. She had a beautiful hazelnut complexion. Her skin was smooth and beautiful. It was even more impressive because she wore no makeup. In that moment, he wanted to reach out and feel her skin.

Suddenly the phone rang.

Morgan put her food down and went to answer it. "Hello, Sheikh Bukhari's office," she answered. She turned swiftly and looked at him with her eyes wide open. She covered the mouthpiece and whispered loudly, "It's your father!"

Chapter 8

Sofian frowned. He was not expecting a call from his father, especially on his work phone on a Saturday. He took a sip of his drink before getting up. Then he walked over to the desk. He took the phone from Morgan.

"Father, is everything alright?" he said into the receiver. Morgan returned to her lunch.

"No son, everything is not well. I have tried your cell phone and house phone," his father replied. Sofian was surprised. His father rarely looked for him. If he needed him, he would simply send his assistant to call.

"My cell phone is on silent." Sofian fished the phone out of his pocket. He unlocked the phone and saw eight missed calls. Something must have been really wrong.

"Son, I need you to come home immediately," his father said. The distress in his voice was clear.

"What happened?"

"It's about your brother." His father paused for a moment.

"What happened to Samir?"

"The Khans, they took him." His father paused again. "He's gone, Sofian." The Khans were a small tribe that resided in the desert.

"What do you mean he is gone?" Sofian asked his father. His father was not articulating himself as well as he normally did. He was beating around the bush, he was nervous and distressed. It was unlike him. Sofian was getting more and more worried.

"He's dead," his father said.

"What?" Sofian spat out. Morgan whipped her head in his direction.

"They killed him."

Sofian was silent, as the words sank in. "Why would the Khans kill Samir?" said Sofian. He knew that the Khans did not like his family because of an old family feud. However he did not think they hated his family enough to kill his brother, the crown prince.

"Son, you need to come home," said his father. "Better to talk in person."

"Okay." Sofian hung up. He and his father weren't much for words. They were not like normal fathers and sons that spend hours together and on the phone. Sofian was a prince and his father was the king.

"Is everything okay?" Morgan asked Sofian.

"No." He shook his head. He stood there looking both confused and sad. "Get my jet ready."

"Okay, to fly where?"

"Back to Kaslan."

"Is everything okay?" Morgan asked again softly as she rose from her seat.

"Just do as I say," Sofian said to her.

Morgan nodded. She quickly cleared up the lunch and left the room. She returned to her desk and did what she was told. She was a bit concerned about Sofian. She had heard him speak about Samir being killed. She wondered who Samir was. She wanted to ask but she was scared of his reaction. After she had called for the jet, she returned to Sofian's office.

"Sir, the jet is being fueled up now and will be ready for takeoff whenever you are ready," Morgan said to him. "I have also called your driver."

Sofian was standing by the window looking outside. He turned and picked up his suit jacket. "Grab all these files and anything you may need," he instructed Morgan. With confusion, she gathered up the files on the desk quickly.

"What should I do with them?" Morgan asked.

"You are to bring them with you."

"Bring them with me?" Morgan mumbled as she stalked Sofian who was walking out.

"You are to come with me."

"To Kaslan?"

"Yes, Morgan," Sofian replied curtly. Morgan rushed to her desk. She locked her computer, grabbed her work laptop and her bag. She ran after Sofian.

"I will need to go home to get some things," Morgan said softly. She spoke gently because she did not want to anger Sofian. He was already sad about someone's death. That someone must have been very important. Important enough for him to return home in a heartbeat.

"I'll get you anything you need there," Sofian said to her. Morgan wanted to protest but she bit her tongue instead. It wasn't like she lived with anyone or anything. She did not have to get permission from anyone. It was an awkward situation for her to be going to a different country with Sofian. It was going to be even more awkward having him buy her things.

Morgan managed to be silent for most of their ride to the airport. However the curiosity was killing her. If she was going to accompany him to his country, she needed to know why.

"Sir, why do you need me to come with you?" she asked quietly.

"You're my assistant." Sofian was looking out of the window.

"Who is Samir?" Morgan spoke as gently as she could. Sofian did not answer straight away. He kept looking out of the window quietly.

"He is my brother," he said at last. Morgan's jaw dropped open. Samir was Sofian's brother, and he had been killed. She was not sure what to do or say. She had never been good at comforting people. With caution, she reached out and placed her hand on his shoulder.

"Was he killed?"

"According to my father."

Morgan rubbed his shoulder. "I'm sorry," she said.

Sofian shook his head. "It's not true. It can't be true." He was in denial. Of course he was. It was not easy to have been told that your brother had been murdered.

"We will be in Kaslan in a few hours, and all your questions will be answered. Is there anything I can do for you now?" Morgan said softly as she rubbed his shoulder. She did not know what else to say.

The car pulled up as they reached the airstrip. Sofian opened the door for himself and got out of the car. He did not even bother to wait for his chauffeur. Morgan opened her door too and followed him out.

The flight attendant was already waiting for them outside the jet. She bowed her head as Sofian

59

approached. He did not even acknowledge it. He climbed the stairs and got into the jet. Morgan smiled and greeted the flight attendant. She returned Morgan's smile and helped her with the files in her hands.

The interior of the jet was mostly white. The leather seats were white, and they had black armrests and black tabletops. Morgan went to sit opposite from Sofian. She placed her handbag next to her. The flight attendant put the files on the table. She offered them refreshments before she left. Sofian shook his head and Morgan followed his lead. They both buckled their seatbelts, ready for takeoff.

Chapter 9

Morgan and Sofian arrived in Kaslan hours later. It was already evening over there. However the sun was still setting. Morgan eyeballed the peach and grey skies as she climbed down the stairs of the jet. Sofian walked in front of her quietly. There was a car already waiting for them. A man dressed smartly in a suit opened the door for them.

It was a short ride to the palace. When the car pulled up, Morgan turned to Sofian. She once again placed her hand on his shoulder. "Are you ready?" she asked him. She instantly regretted the words. How could he be ready?

"As ready as I can be," Sofian said. The chauffeur opened the door for Sofian. He stepped out of the car. Morgan instantly followed him out.

The maids bowed their heads to Sofian as he walked into the palace. Sofian said something to one of the maids in Arabic. She nodded and then asked Morgan to go with her. Sofian walked off in the other direction.

Sofian rushed to his parents' quarters. As he walked, he felt as though he was never going to get there. The distance he had walked so many times now felt like miles. He hoped that when he arrived, what he had heard on the phone would not be true. He so badly hoped that his brother was still alive.

"Sheikh Sofian has arrived," the maid outside his parents' quarters announced. He walked into their quarters. He found his father sitting in the living room with a glass of whiskey in his hand. His father rarely drank alcoholic beverages. Sofian walked over to wooden shelf with all the alcoholic drinks. He took a glass and also poured himself some whiskey.

"Father, I am here," Sofian said as he joined his father and sat down in a chair. His father looked up and nodded. He took a sip of whiskey.

"Everything is a mess right now," his father said. He looked so distraught.

"Where is mother?"

"In her office, sorting everything out for the funeral. She's been keeping herself busy. If she becomes idle, even for a second, she breaks down."

Sofian nodded. It was much like his mother. "What exactly happened to Samir? How did it happen?" Sofian took a sip of his drink.

His father shrugged his shoulders. "Samir was in the desert visiting the small tribes. That's when the Khans attacked him and –" His father stopped speaking. The words were too difficult to get out. There was a long silence between Sofian and his father. Neither one of them was good at expressing emotions.

Sofian had been raised as a prince. His childhood was unlike other children's childhoods. His parents had not raised him. They had national and internationals matters to attend to. He spent most of his time in books and not outside like other kids. There hadn't been any time for him to develop emotional bonds with his parents.

"Have you caught them?" Sofian asked his father.

"Some of them," his father replied.

"Some." Sofian gulped down all of his whiskey. He banged the glass onto the table, causing it to smash into pieces. His father almost jumped out of his skin. "I will find every single one of them. And I will annihilate the entire clan."

Sofian felt so much rage flowing through him. He got up and walked out of the room. He so badly wanted to catch the killers of his brother. They had to pay for what they had done. With blood dripping from his hand, he swore to avenge his brother's death.

Morgan was just standing in the doorway to her room speaking to a maid when she saw Sofian walking into his chambers. Morgan was to stay in the room across from Sofian's. She noticed that his hand was bleeding. She quickly followed him.

Morgan caught up with him in his living room. She stood in front of him. She wanted to ask him if he was okay, but of course he was not okay. There was no point in asking fruitless questions. "What happened to your hand?" she asked.

"Not now, Morgan, return to your room," he instructed her and walked out of the room. Two maids walked into the living room.

"Can you get a first-aid kit for me, please?" Morgan asked them. They looked at each other. "Please hurry, thank you."

Morgan headed out of the living room and followed Sofian's footsteps. Probably not one of her best ideas. She suddenly found herself walking into his bathroom where he was. Sofian ran his hand through his hair and then punched the mirror. Morgan gasped. She rushed to his side and took his hand.

"Hurting yourself won't help," she said.

"Did I not tell you to return to your chambers?" he shouted at her. Morgan had never seen him so angry and so hurt. She opened the tap and let the cold water run. She cautiously took his wrist and put his hand under the cold water.

"What are you doing?" he asked her.

"Cleaning your cuts," she said.

"Excuse me," the maid said, so quietly. She stood in the doorway holding the first-aid kit. "I brought the kit."

"Bring it here," Morgan replied. She rushed in and gave Morgan the kit, then rushed back out. Morgan opened the kit and pulled out tweezers. She inspected Sofian's cuts and pulled out pieces of glass in them. Sofian watched her with his eyebrows crossed.

"I don't know what you're going through. I don't know what to say to make you feel better," Morgan said to him. She took a cotton swab and put some antiseptic on it. She used it to clean Sofian's cuts. "Just don't hurt yourself," she said. After cleaning his cuts, she bandaged his hand.

When she was done, she took the kit and walked out of his quarters. There was nothing much she could do for him. It was not like they were friends. If they were, then she would have hugged him. Bandaging his hand and leaving him to mourn in peace was all she could do.

Morgan headed back to her luxurious quarters. As she walked in, there were expensive chairs that surrounded a wooden table with an intricate design. The floors were made of the finest marble. Her four-poster bed was quite high. The bedroom itself was twice the size of her bedroom in the States. It felt like she was living in a high-class hotel. She fished her phone out of her bag and Skype called Brooke.

"Why are you calling me on Skype?" Brooke said as she answered. They normally texted each other or called on the phone and not on Skype.

"Look where I am." Morgan had Brook on video call. She started showing Brooke the bedroom.

"Where are you?" Brooke leaned into the camera.

"In Kaslan."

"What? Why are you there?"

"I came with the sheikh." Morgan threw herself on the bed.

"Is that why he called you into work on a Saturday?" Brooke asked.

"No, his brother died. So he came as soon as he found out. I feel so bad for him," Morgan replied.

"Really? Bless him."

"I know."

"So what is the purpose of you being there?"

"He just said I had to come because I was his assistant. I guess he wants to make sure that I carry on working."

"That makes no sense. He just wanted you with him."

"I don't like where this is going. I am tired. I am going to sleep."

Brooke laughed. "Okay, call me tomorrow then," she said.

"I will." Morgan ended the call. She placed her cell phone on the nightstand and got in under the covers.

Chapter 10

Sofian approached his mother and Zara, Samir's wife, at the church where they were holding the funeral for his brother. He kissed his mother on both cheeks. "Why are you late?" she asked him.

"I just had matters to attend to," he replied. He had sent some specially trained men to the desert. He needed them to find all of the Khans, the entire tribe. They were all going to pay for his brother's death. He took Zara's hands into his and kissed her on both cheeks.

"How are you holding up?" he asked her.

"As well as I can," she said and forced a smile.

"What happened to your hand?" his mother asked. She took his wrist and inspected his hand.

"It's nothing." He inspected his right hand. Morgan had bandaged it for him. It was very strange. No one had done that for him before. Whenever he had gotten hurt in the past, it was always a doctor or nurse that did it but never someone without medical experience. Despite him shouting at Morgan, she still dared to touch him.

People approached him and his mother and Zara to say their condolences. His mother did most of the talking. Sofian did not know what he was to say to them. It was polite for people to give their condolences but he could not do anything with condolences. They did not make him feel better and they did not bring back the dead.

"Sir." Sofian heard a quiet voice. He turned and saw Morgan standing there in her black dress. "I didn't know if I was to come or not."

"It's fine," Sofian replied. He felt strangely relieved to have her there. She was the only one not looking at him with a sad face and pretending to care. Most of the people at the funeral did not know Samir personally. There were governors, ministers, princes, princesses, sheikhs and kings from different places. They were only there out of courtesy.

"Do you need me to do anything?" Morgan asked him.

"No, just stand there," he replied.

"Sofian," his mother began to say. She paused when she saw Morgan. "Who is she?"

"My assistant."

"Hello, my name is Morgan," she introduced herself. "I am so sorry about your son."

Sofian's mother nodded. "Thank you," she said. She looked at Sofian. "We need to take our seats," she said to him.

"Where is father?" Sofian asked.

"Speaking with an envoy from Lebanon."

Sofian nodded. He gently placed his hand on his mother's back and went with her to sit down. Morgan followed quietly. The four of them sat down at the front of the church. Moments later, Sofian's father came to join them. He sat next to his wife.

Sofian was sad and relieved when the funeral ended. He no longer wanted to be around all the people. He felt very sad after seeing his brother's body. He had not even gotten a chance to say goodbye. The last time they had spoken, they had had a normal conversation. It angered him that he could no longer speak to his brother or see him or hang out with him.

"Let's all eat together," said Sofian's mother when they returned home. She sounded and looked exhausted. It was understandable. It had been a long morning and afternoon. Her husband put his arm around her and headed to the dining room with her. Zara had left and gone to her quarters. She did not really want to be around people.

"I'll see you soon," Morgan said to Sofian. She turned on her heel to leave. Sofian grabbed hold of her dress and pulled her back. "Sofian!" she shouted. He raised his eyebrows.

"You are calling me by my name now," he said to her.

"That was a slip." She cleared her throat. "Never mind that. Why are you dragging me backwards?"

"My mother said we should eat together."

"I did not think she meant me also."

"It does not matter either way. You must come."

"Why?"

"Because I said so." Sofian was not going to explain himself to her. Her being around him was strangely calming.

"Okay." Morgan crossed her eyebrows. Sofian started walking towards the dining room. Morgan followed. They joined his parents at the dining table.

"How long have you worked for my son?" Sofian's mother asked Morgan.

"I was a research assistant for months but I became his assistant about a month ago," Morgan replied. Sofian raised an eyebrow. Morgan could have just said *a month*. However she was a talkative girl.

"How is it going?" Sofian's father asked Morgan.

"It's interesting, I must say. I have never worked in this kind of role before but I quickly got the hang of it," she replied.

His father smiled at her. "So by interesting, you mean to say that you like it?"

"The interesting thing is Sofian, I mean Sheikh Sofian, Prince Sofian? I never know what the best way to address him is. Anyway he is hard to read, and a bit fussy at times." Morgan laughed a little. His father laughed with her. Sofian shook his head. Because Morgan spoke too much, she often said a lot of unnecessary things. The maids brought in the food and started serving them.

"I am never fussy," Sofian protested.

"You are," said his mother. She offered a warm smile. After the maids had finished dishing out the food, they all started eating.

"The crown prince's position is now empty," said Sofian's father. Everyone immediately turned serious. "Sofian, you will have to fill it."

Sofian jerked his head up and looked at his father. "Father, we only just buried Samir," he spat out. The last thing on his mind was the throne. Not once in his life had he ever considered the crown. It was always Samir's.

"I am aware of that but this was inevitable. It is best we discuss it as soon as possible. That position cannot be empty."

Sofian closed his eyes momentarily. He had not even finished mourning his brother. How could he think of taking his position? Sofian dropped his fork.

"I don't want it," he said.

"Perhaps we can talk about this another time," his mother said softly. Sofian shook his head.

"There is no one else. Sofian, you have to be the future king of Kaslan," said his father. Sofian pulled his chair back and stood up. He walked out of the room.

Chapter 11

Morgan had never felt so awkward in her life. She was left sitting at the table with Sofian's parents. She did not know whether she should follow Sofian out or just sit there. She should not have been there when they discussed making Sofian the crown prince. She could understand why he was resisting.

She looked at his parents. His mother looked sympathetic towards Sofian. She sighed and looked at her husband. "We should have waited to speak to him about it," she said to him.

"Perhaps. However Samir was due to take the throne soon. So we need to prepare Sofian as soon as possible," the king replied. He was so majestic and elegant. Morgan had never been in the presence of a king before. She itched to ask him why Samir was to take the throne soon. Usually the crown prince became king after the king died, unless he abdicated. To Morgan the king still looked capable to be king.

"Morgan, it was nice to meet you. I have to go lie down. Please excuse me," the queen said as she stood up from her chair.

"The pleasure was all mine," Morgan said to her. She smiled at Morgan warmly and left. Now things were even more awkward. Morgan was left sitting with the king. He called a maid over and asked her to bring him whiskey.

"Things are falling apart," he said. Morgan was not sure if he was speaking to her. He was not looking at her. He had his head buried in his hands. She was not sure what to say to him, so she just stayed quietly. The maid came with tray containing a bottle of whiskey and several glasses. She poured whiskey into a glass for him and set down the tray on the table.

The king sighed heavily before he took a sip. "I can't even mourn my son properly because I am a king," he said.

"What do you mean?" Morgan asked.

"As a king you cannot show useless things such as emotions. It makes you look weak. And now I have to force my other son to be the crown prince." The king shook his head and drank some more.

"Showing emotion does not make you look weak."

The king smiled. "As a king it does. If you show your weakness, then your enemies will use it against you," he said.

"Maybe. This time your eldest son has passed on. You are allowed to mourn him," she replied. The king finished his whiskey. He took the bottle and poured himself some more.

"Shall I drink with you?" Morgan asked. The king poured her a glass.

"It's strange how things change just like that."

Morgan took a sip of the whiskey. The taste was so strong, she almost spat it out. The drink burned her throat as she swallowed it. She frowned and started coughing. She spilled some of it on her dress as she was coughing. The king started laughing. "I am so sorry," she said.

"It's an acquired taste. Not everyone can appreciate its taste," he said. He started laughing again.

"It's so strong." Morgan preferred something sweeter to drink. "I am not a drinker."

"It shows."

"Can I ask one question?"

"Ask."

"Why are you abdicating?" Morgan asked. "That's too personal, isn't it? You don't have to answer. Forget my words."

"I'm diabetic," the king said. "Unfortunately, my illness is not well controlled by medication."

Morgan gasped. "I am so sorry to hear that."

"Don't be. I now get tired quicker and sometimes I feel too unwell to travel."

Morgan nodded. It made sense. He would need to rest and take it easy. "I can understand that," she said. She stayed with the king a little while longer. He drank his whiskey and she snacked on anything she could get her hands on. After he was too drunk, she asked the maids to escort him back to his room. She stood up and headed back to her quarters.

Morgan walked into her quarters and took her shoes off. She touched her belly. She was so full. She had eaten so much. She let her curls down. As she was about to sit down, she decided to go check on Sofian. She wondered how he was, especially since he had walked out during lunch.

"Where is the sheikh?" Morgan asked one of the maids as she walked into Sofian's quarters.

"In his bedchamber," the maids replied. Morgan nodded and headed that way. His quarters were much bigger than hers obviously. The floors were also made of marble. She knocked on his bedroom room.

"Yes," he called out. Morgan grabbed the golden handle and slid the door open. Sofian was lying on his back. Morgan approached him.

"I came to check on you," she said.

"Oh, it's you," he said.

"Great welcome. Makes me feel warm and fuzzy inside."

"I'm just being my usual fussy self."

Morgan's jaw hung open. His tone was so serious, she could not tell if he was joking or not. "Are you mad about that?" she asked. It seemed as though he was upset about her calling him fussy earlier.

"I am not *mad* about anything," he said the word with so much sarcasm. Morgan went to sit down on the bed next to him. She could not help but notice how massive his bed was. It could fit ten people on it.

"Morgan, what are you up to?" he asked her.

"I am not up to anything. Why would you think that?" she replied.

He sat up and looked at her with a raised eyebrow. "You are in my bed."

Morgan narrowed her gaze at him and shook her head. She knew what he was trying to suggest. "The maids got this dress for me," she said, changing the subject. Sofian looked at it. He frowned a little.

"It does nothing for your curves," he pointed out. Morgan raised her eyebrows. He had even noticed her "curves"?

"That was not the aim." She was only looking for something to wear at the funeral. She was not trying to impress anyone.

"You smell like alcohol."

"Your dad was drinking whiskey and I thought I would drink with him. However it tasted awful." Morgan frowned as she recalled the taste.

"You drank with the king?" Sofian was shocked.

"Yes. He even poured it for me." Morgan wiggled her eyebrows. "In Korea, it was considered an impossible honor for the king to pour a drink for a peasant like me."

"You say a lot of weird things." Sofian smiled and shook his head.

"I don't say weird things!"

Sofian raised his eyebrows. He obviously did not believe her. Morgan rose to her feet. "I am going to lie down," she said to him as she rubbed her belly.

"It's still early."

"I'm not tired, just really full."

"Not only do you say weird things, you do weird things."

Morgan shook her head. She turned to leave but once again Sofian grabbed her dress. "Again?" She cried out.

"Stay," he said. He let go of her dress and lay back down on the bed.

"What?" Morgan asked.

"Stay, here."

Chapter 12

Sofian moved over, creating space for Morgan. She got on the bed and lay down next to him. It was a weird request. He did not know why, but her presence was comforting. Her weirdness distracted him from feeling too sad.

"Your bed is so comfortable," she said.

Sofian smiled to himself. "Glad you are comfortable," he replied lazily.

Morgan rolled over to her side and looked at him. "Are you going to do it, become the crown prince?"

Sofian sighed heavily. That was one thing he did not want to speak about. "You're too noisy," he said.

"It might be not a bad thing."

"What!" Sofian looked fiercely at her.

"Hear me out," she said. "If you don't do it, then who will? Isn't it better that you do it? Someone who was close to Samir. I am sure he would rather you take his place than someone else."

Sofian looked away. He had not thought of it that way. Her words made so much sense. When had she gotten so wise and good with words? "Maybe," he said at last.

Morgan started drawing on his shoulder with her finger. "Guess what I am writing," she said.

"Just when I start to think you are normal, you do something even weirder."

"Argh." Morgan made an odd sound and turned to face the other side. Sofian just smiled to himself.

"You're such a bore," she complained.

***

Morgan slowly opened her eyes. She was so sleepy that it was almost impossible to open them. She brushed her hair out of her face. She stretched her arms. She let out a squeak as she stretched. Stretching felt so good.

"You're awake," Sofian said.

Morgan rolled over and looked at him. She had forgotten where she was. She sat up instantly. Sofian was sitting up. He was leaning against the headboard, and reading a book.

"I fell asleep?" Morgan asked. She couldn't believe that she had fallen asleep in his bed. She always found it difficult to sleep in new places, and yet she had slept so comfortably and easily in Sofian's bed.

"You snore."

"I do not!"

"You are so defensive."

"I am not." After saying the words, Morgan realized that she was being defensive. She actually was defensive. She rolled her eyes. "What is the time?"

"It's just after ten."

"Huh? Did I sleep that long?"

"You did."

Morgan got out of Sofian's bed. "I am leaving," she said and rushed out of the room. She felt a little embarrassed. She wondered if she had talked in her sleep. She had a tendency to do that. Then her hair, it was always messy when she woke up. She could not believe that she had fallen asleep in front of him. It was not even in front of him, it was next to him.

Morgan shut the door behind her when she got into her own bedroom. She unzipped her dress and climbed into bed. It had been a long and strange day for her. She needed to close her eyes and just relax.

The next morning, Morgan had her breakfast in her quarters. She sat at the luxurious chairs and just soaked in the warm sun seeping through the windows. It was nice to have breakfast brought to her. She took her laptop and just started looking over some work documents. She thought that she might as well work.

"Miss," one of the maids said as she approached Morgan.

"Hi." Morgan smiled at her.

"The sheikh bought you some things."

"Like what?" Morgan turned her head. She saw two maids walk into the room with a rack of clothes. Other maids followed with shopping bags. "What's all this?" she asked.

"The sheikh said to get you clothes and other feminine things, since you left the States without anything," the leader of the maids said.

Morgan rose to her feet with her jaw hung open. "I just have to pick a few items, yes?" she asked.

"Everything here is for you. Please have a look and let us know if there is anything else you wish to have," the maid said to her. Morgan was speechless. Sofian had basically gotten her a whole new wardrobe.

Morgan walked over to the rack. She touched different colored fabrics. There were different styles of clothing. Dresses, skirts, blouses, shorts, trousers. All different colors. There was an outfit for every occasion. She looked in the shopping bags. There were different kinds of shoes, lingerie, toiletries, makeup, hair accessories and even nail varnishes.

She was speechless. She only needed a few outfits and toiletries. Sofian had gone above and beyond. She wondered if Sofian had simply asked the maids to get her clothes or if he had told them specifically what to give her. The more time she spent with him the more she could not figure him out. On a bright note, she was witnessing different sides of him, which made it easier for her to be around him and to deal with him.

Morgan decided to go see Sofian. His maids looked at her as she walked in. One of them tried to stop her. "Miss, you cannot just walk in here without receiving permission from the sheikh," she said to her.

"I come in here all the time. It's never been an issue," Morgan said to her. Actually, she had come there a few times, and not all the time. Still, the point was the same. Sofian had never given her backlash for it.

"Let me tell him you're here first."

"Don't worry about it." Morgan walked in anyway. Life in the palace was different from what she was used to. There were maids everywhere. She had to think twice before doing anything reckless. Morgan heard the maids calling after her but she ignored them. She kept walking and checking each room for him.

"Morgan," Sofian said without looking up from his newspaper to her as she walked into the room he was sitting in. It was beautifully furnished with black-and-white furniture which matched the curtains. The floors were made of white marble. There was a nice fireplace that complemented the room.

"Sheikh Sofian, we tried to stop her," the maid that had spoken to Morgan said to Sofian. He dismissed her with his hand.

"It's fine. Leave us," he said to her. The maid bowed her head and left the room.

"I have not seen her before," Morgan said to Sofian.

"She was not on duty for the past few days, I believe. I am surprised that she did not tackle you to stop you from coming in."

Morgan raised her eyebrows. "Why would she?" Was that another one of his odd jokes? He'd say a joke with a straight face.

"Normally you cannot just come in here without my say-so. She usually makes sure that no one enters."

"Oh, I was too fast for her." Morgan gaped at everything in the room. "What is this room?"

"Drawing room."

"Drawing room? That's so ancient." The drawing room was a room rich people had in their homes centuries ago. Its purpose was to entertain guests before dinner, sort of like a living room. Morgan did not even understand why it was called a drawing room and why people had it.

"Something I can help you with?" Sofian asked with half a smile on his face.

"I've seen the boutique you had sent to me," Morgan said as she sat down. He was sitting on a chair. She sat on the settee to his right.

"I don't know what you speak of."

"All the things you bought for me are enough to outfit a boutique."

"Oh." Sofian flipped the newspaper page. "Are they to your liking?"

"If I said no?"

"More things can be bought for you."

Morgan shook her head. "No more Sofi–Sheikh Sofian." She cleared her throat. Lately whenever she tried addressing him, his first name seemed to slip out of her mouth instead of sir, sheikh or your highness. Sofian looked up from his newspaper.

"I am just saying that you got me far more than I need," she said. He looked down at the newspaper.

"I have never heard a woman say that," he said lazily.

"It's too much. You have to take some of it back."

"Never heard that either."

Morgan narrowed her gaze at him. He was not taking her seriously. She shook her head. "What will you do today?" she asked him. He looked up again.

"Is this your way of asking to spend some quality time with me?" he said. Again his tone was so serious.

However Morgan knew what he was thinking. He was joking with her.

"Yes," she said. She went along with his joke.

"Do as you please."

When he did not react, it sucked all the fun out of it. "No thank you, I have work to do." She rose to her feet and headed out of the room.

"Do you really think I should be the crown prince?" Sofian called out after Morgan. She stopped and looked at him. She smiled and nodded. "It's okay to take Samir's place?"

"Don't think of it as taking his place. Rather finishing his work." Morgan smiled and walked out.

Chapter 13

Sofian went to meet with his father. After really thinking about it, and listening to Morgan, he decided to accept the position. He did not have much choice anyway. He did not have any other brothers. He was the only one left to do it. He was just being his stubborn self. He adjusted his tie before walking into the king's office.

"I trust that you are well, Father," Sofian said.

"I am," his father replied. He gestured for Sofian to sit down.

"I won't take up too much of your time." Sofian cleared his throat. "I will do as you say."

His father nodded. "It's the only thing to do, son," his father said.

Sofian knew that already. However, where was he to begin? He knew nothing about being the crown prince. He had gone off to the U.S. to live life the way he wanted. He had focused on growing the family business and he had been incredibly successful. That was what he knew, not this.

"It won't be easy," Sofian said.

"No, it won't be. We have to start preparing you now," his father replied. Sofian bowed his head to his father and headed out of the room. He already knew the chaos that awaited him. He had watched his brother go through it. There were to be endless sessions on politics and economics. He had to learn about all the other countries. A king should never be in a position where he lacked knowledge.

He walked into his quarters and headed to his office. He told one of the maids to summon Morgan. Just because he was in Kaslan did not mean that he had to stop working. He needed to check on everything that was happening in the States.

Sofian sat in his white leather chair. It felt like he had not been in his home office for so long. He looked up. There was a photo of him and Samir on the wall. He banged his fist on the table. He needed the Khans caught quickly. It was taking longer than he had anticipated. There was a knock on the door. Morgan walked into the room.

"Did you ask for me?" she said.

"Would the maid have said so if I had not told her to?" he spat out. Morgan frowned. Sofian knew that he had scared her. She had only asked a simple question. She was not really asking, it was her basically announcing her arrival. He instantly felt bad. She did not deserve that.

"I did not mean to snap at you. I just have a lot on my mind," he said to her. He rubbed his forehead. Morgan sat on the chair opposite him.

"I understand," she said softly. She reached out and took his hands into hers. Sofian was not expecting that at all. Her tiny hands were so soft and warm. She had said to him that she was not good at comforting people, and yet she was doing a good job comforting him.

"You're holding my hands," he said to her.

"I know. Apparently it's a way to comfort people. Is it working?"

Sofian almost burst into laughter. She was funny and she did not even know it. "I went to see my father," he said changing the subject, and not letting go of her hands either.

"How did that go?"

Sofian sighed before he replied. "We did not talk for long. For the first time in my life I'm not confident I can do this," he said.

Morgan smiled. She did not look shocked. "The things that matter scare us," she said.

"What?"

"It's a big thing to be crown prince. You have a lot of work ahead of you."

"You are really helping here," he said sarcastically. Morgan laughed. He let go of her hands and crossed his eyebrows. It only made her laugh instead.

"If it doesn't challenge you then it won't change you."

"Do you have any more motivational quotes?"

"Go hard or go home." Morgan grinned. Sofian looked puzzled. He did not understand that quote. "My point is this is a good thing. Things that are challenging are good things. I think you will be good at it, once you get the hang of it."

"You have faith in me?"

"I do." Morgan smiled. "So what do you need me to do?"

"Send out an email to everyone informing them that I will be here for a while."

"I have already done so. I told them to forward their reports to you or to me."

Sofian nodded. He liked her using her initiative. "Okay. I also need you to finish the paperwork for the child-friendly painkiller," he said.

"I have finished with it. I did the research for the ingredients, I did a preliminary budget list and everything else you asked," Morgan said.

Sofian stroked his chin. He was very impressed. He knew he had made the right decision in hiring her.

She was proving him right. "I'm now left not knowing what to tell you do," Sofian said to her.

Morgan laughed. "I am good at my job."

"You are."

"Thank you. That is the closest you've been to complimenting me. I'll take it."

Sofian smiled. "Well, just keep watch of your email. Look over all reports sent to you." Sofian could not think of anything else to make her do. It was odd. Normally he gave his assistants tons of work to do. His mind was too consumed with this crown prince business.

"I will do so," Morgan replied.

"I will summon you when I have more for you to do." Sofian dismissed her.

Morgan laughed. "Summon," she repeated. "It's such an odd word. I don't think people really use that."

"I do," said Sofian. There was nothing wrong with using the word summon.

"No, I mean normal people. Us peasants." She bowed her head and left the room. That was the first time she had bowed her head to him. He was not sure if it was legit or she was being sarcastic about it.

Chapter 14

Morgan sat in her quarters dealing with emails from workers, just as Sofian had asked. She had never been so idle since she had started working for Sofian. He always had a lot of things for her to do. She looked at her hands. She could not believe that she had held his hands. It was so out of her character. It was even more surprising that he had let her do so.

A maid knocked on her bedroom door. "Miss, lunch is ready," she said.

"Okay," Morgan called out. She felt so pampered. All her meals were prepared for her. Clothes and shoes had been bought for her. She got up from her bed and took her laptop with her.

The table had already been set for her. The cooks had prepared rice, lamb, Mediterranean salad and pita bread. Morgan's mouth instantly watered. She sat down at the table. She flipped open her laptop. She decided to call Brooke on Skype while she ate. It was still morning in the States. Brooke must have been getting ready for work.

"It's too early to talk," Brooke said as she answered her Skype.

"Good morning to you too," Morgan replied.

"Hurry up and tell me the gossip. As you know, I have work soon."

"What gossip? I am just calling to see how you are," she lied. She needed to tell her about everything that been going on with Sofian.

"Hey. Right now you need to tell me what's been going on over there."

"You tell me what's been going on there."

"The usual. Everyone is talking about you."

"Still? They need to get over it. I was only made an assistant and nothing special."

"Nothing special? You are working with the sheikh and now you are in Kaslan. Everyone is talking about you being in Kaslan. I guess they're just jealous."

Morgan bit into her succulent lamb. Brooke stared into the camera. "Are you eating? Hurry up and tell me the gossip. I have no time!" she shouted. Morgan burst into laughter and almost spat out her meat.

"Okay," she said. She quickly chewed and swallowed. "I went to the funeral, drank whiskey with the king, I slept in Sofian's bed, he bought me tons of clothes and shoes, he has to be the crown prince now obviously, I held his hands this morning and that's everything." She spoke so fast, she was out of breath when she was done. ,

"My head is spinning right now," said Brooke. She was just staring into the camera with her jaw hung open. "I don't even know where to begin," Brooke continued.

"That's everything," Morgan said and grinned.

"This is worth being late for." Brooke cleared her throat. "You slept in Sofian's bed?"

"Get your mind out of the gutter. Nothing like that happened." Morgan quickly explained the full situation to her. It did not seem to make much of a difference to Brooke.

"Just what is going on between you and the sheikh?"

"Nothing. I am just his assistant."

"The pair of you are in love with each other but no one will admit it first," Brooke teased.

Morgan almost choked on her drink. "Love? You need to get to work," said Morgan.

"One day, you will tell me how your love has blossomed."

"There won't be such a day. I am now hanging up on you now. My food is getting cold and you are running late," Morgan said to Brooke.

"I'll be waiting for the–" Before Brooke could finish speaking Morgan ended the call. She knew what Brooke was going to say and she was trying not to hear it. There was nothing between her and Sofian.

She was just his assistant. He looked at her as just an assistant and she looked at him as just her boss. That was all there was to it.

After Morgan had finished eating, she sorted out Sofian's schedule for the week. He had a very busy week ahead of him. He was to meet with different people who were going to help him prepare for the throne. They would more or less tutor him. She suddenly wondered what Sofian was doing. She wanted to go check but she stopped herself.

***

Sofian attended his first meeting as crown prince. Each week, the king attended a cabinet meeting with all the ministers and his advisers. When the crown prince reached a certain age, he had to attend cabinet meetings also. When Sofian and his father entered the room, the ministers rose from their seats and bowed their heads.

The ministers waited for the king and Sofian to sit down before they did. They were sitting at an oval shaped table with the king at one end and Sofian at the other.

"It's good to see you, Sheikh Sofian," one of the ministers said to him.

"It is indeed. You have grown up really well," another minister agreed with him.

"Thank you," Sofian replied.

The secretary of state read out the minutes from the previous meeting. Sofian looked at his hand. He still had the bandage on. The bandage that Morgan had wrapped around his hand. In a way she was motherly. She had taken care of him in her own way. It was odd. No one had ever taken care of him like that.

Sofian found himself remembering Morgan in his bed. She slept so peacefully. She looked so adorable, and she had spoken in her sleep. He wondered if she was liking it in Kaslan, and if she was comfortable. Sofian shook his head. There was no time to be thinking about Morgan. He was in an important meeting.

"The last thing we need to discuss is the coronation," said the secretary of state.

"Yes, we need to do one at the right time. If we do it too early, it seems insensitive to the previous crown prince. However if we take too long, the people will be uncomfortable knowing that the crown prince position is empty," said one of the ministers.

"You are right," said the king. Sofian said nothing. Everything was just happening too quickly. He wished that he would not have a coronation. However that was not up to him. Even if they listened to him and did not do one, there would be so much speculation.

"However let us discuss that at a further time," said the king as he rose from his chair. Sofian also stood up.

"Yes, your highness," the ministers said as they rose from their seats also. They bowed their heads as Sofian and the king left the room.

"So how was your first cabinet meeting?" the king asked his son when they were out of the conference room.

"It was what I expected," Sofian said. He had found it incredibly boring.

"And what did you expect?"

"I expected it to be so uninteresting."

The king laughed. "You will get used to it, son," he said. Sofian shrugged his shoulders in response. "By the way, how is your assistant?" he asked.

Sofian looked at his father with a puzzled expression. "Morgan? Why would you ask about her?" Sofian asked. It was rather strange that his father was asking about Morgan. He had never asked about Sofian's employees before.

"She left an impression on me."

"She did?"

"Yes. She's very talkative," the king said. *Tell me about it,* Sofian thought to himself. "But it's good. She is full of life and very entertaining," his father continued.

"She is something," said Sofian. "I am off to start my foreign affairs meeting." Sofian bowed his head to his father.

"Okay, I will see you soon." The king smiled and walked off.

Chapter 15

Morgan accompanied Sofian to a tent meeting. A tent meeting was a just a meeting where the king would meet up with sheikhs from different tribes and neighboring countries. The tent meeting was first done in the 1900s. The sheikhs would meet in a tent. That was where the name was generated. Now they met in the Kaslan Empire Hotel. Samir had been going to the meetings in place of his father. Now it was Sofian who had to do it.

"Are you nervous about the tent meeting?" Morgan asked Sofian. "Your first ever." She emphasized the fact that it was his first meeting.

Sofian crossed his eyebrows and looked at her. "I don't get nervous," he said.

Morgan made a sound. "If you say so."

"My father asked about you."

"Did he?" Morgan's eyes flew open. "When was this?"

"A few days ago."

"And you're just telling me now?"

Sofian crossed his eyebrows at Morgan again. She cleared her throat and looked away. "I did not think it was that important," he said to her. Sofian's phone vibrated. He pulled it out of his pocket and looked at the screen. He grunted and then put the phone back in his pocket.

"Everything okay?" Morgan asked him. He just dismissed the topic with his hand.

"We are here," Sofian said as the car pulled up. The chauffeur got out of the car and opened the door for them. Sofian got out of the car first and then Morgan got out after him.

There were so many officers and soldiers outside the hotel. Sofian had his own personal security detail that tailed him everywhere he went. He went about his business without noticing them. Morgan was not used to them. She and Sofian walked into the hotel.

The hotel was so extravagant. The reception area alone was impressive. There was a long black desk with ten receptionists behind it, each one with their own space. The receptionists were dressed so elegantly. The floor was made of white and black marble tiles. There was a massive crystal chandelier hanging from the ceiling.

One of the receptionists rushed from behind the desk to welcome Sofian. She then escorted him and Morgan into the elevator. The meeting was being held on the Presidential Floor. The receptionist used her key for them to gain access to that floor. No one could get to that floor without a key.

"Miss, you will need to wait for the sheikh in a different room," the receptionist said to Morgan.

"Why?" Morgan asked her.

"Only the sheikhs attend the meeting," Sofian said to her.

"I can't come in?"

"No."

"Only men?" Morgan asked.

"Yes," Sofian replied.

Morgan shrugged her shoulders and just followed the receptionist to the room she was to wait for Sofian in. As she walked there, she wondered why he had brought her to the meeting if she was not even going to attend.

Morgan was served with delicious cold beverages as she waited for Sofian. Fortunately for her there was a television and some magazines in the room. It kept her occupied until Sofian returned. He stood in the doorway and just looked at her.

"What?" Morgan asked him. He had a habit of just staring at her and not saying anything. It was rather odd. She rose from her feet and walked towards him. "How was the meeting?" she asked him.

"Fine, I guess," he replied.

"You guess?" Morgan stood in front of him. He still stared at her with an intense gaze as always. It was so hard to maintain eye contact because he was impossibly handsome.

"My mind was occupied." he said.

"By what?" Morgan knew she should not have asked. He was probably thinking about his brother. Sofian, being his unpredictable self, surprised Morgan by snaking his arm around her and pulling her closer to him. Morgan gasped as she flew into his arms.

Morgan felt incredibly awkward. Here she was standing in Sofian's arms. He had pulled her in but she had not objected. He smelled so good and looked so good. He dipped his head and pressed a kiss against Morgan's lips. She gasped as his lips touched her. Her brain said to push him away and ask what he was doing.

Sofian's lips were soft and felt so good against Morgan's lips. Morgan inhaled his manly scent and let out a small moan. Sofian had his hands on Morgan's lower back. He pulled her closer to him.

Sofian broke off the kiss and just gazed into her eyes. Morgan wanted to protest when he stopped, but she realized where they were. "What are you doing?" she asked and gently pushed him away.

"Kissing you," he replied with a tone that suggested that she had asked the dumbest question.

"Yes, I know that but not here." Morgan created some distance between them. She needed that distance. Her hormones were going crazy. Sofian said nothing. He just stared at her. "If you are finished, we should go," Morgan said and walked out of the room. Her shoulder rubbed Sofian's shoulder as she walked out. She cleared her throat and tried to act as though it did not affect her.

Morgan opened the car door for herself. She did not even wait for the chauffeur to open it for her. She quickly got in and fanned herself. She needed to catch her breath and just comprehend what had just happened.

Sofian joined her in the car moments later. He looked fine. He appeared unaffected. He checked his watch. "Do I have anything else planned for the rest of the day?" he asked her. He was back to normal, as if he had not kissed her. Morgan was confused.

"Just lunch with your mother," Morgan said to him. Sofian just nodded.

The rest of the drive to the palace was a quiet one. Morgan looked out of the window and stared at the palm trees lining the highway. Kaslan was beautiful. She felt sad knowing that she would have to return to the States at some point. She wanted to stay a bit longer and just enjoy the good weather and food.

When they arrived at the palace, Sofian and Morgan went their separate ways. She was to have a conference call with the rest of the managers back in the States. They needed to update her with reports on current projects. Sofian went to have lunch with his mother.

Chapter 16

Sofian kissed his mother on both cheeks before he sat down at the table with her. She was already waiting for him. They were to have lunch together in the palace courtyard. The family often had lunch, dinner or even events in the palace courtyard.

"How was the tent meeting?" his mother asked him.

"It was fine," Sofian replied. He picked up his cutlery and dug into his rice.

"Once you have learned everything and had your coronation, everything will settle down."

"I know. I just have to bear with it all."

"There is something else I wish to discuss with you."

Sofian stopped eating and looked at his mother. Her tone suggested that it was a sensitive topic she was about to approach. "What is it?" he asked.

"For the coronation, you need to have a crown princess," she said. Sofian started eating again. He was not particularly keen on the idea. His mother had picked Zara for Samir. Zara was a good woman. However Sofian did not want a wife arranged for him. He was not even sure he liked the idea of marriage.

"I suppose you already have matches for me," he said to his mother.

"I do." She smiled and pulled some pictures out of her purse. She arranged them on the table for Sofian to see. He looked at them. They were beautiful but not interesting. Nothing about them intrigued Sofian.

He already knew what kind of women they would be. They would not be as funny as Morgan. She was funny and she was very intriguing. They all had perfectly straight silky hair. He used to find it attractive. Now it was just plain to him. Morgan had thick curly coils of hair full of character and life. When she was sleeping in his bed, her hair was so messy. He just wanted to run his hands through it.

"What are you thinking?" his mother asked him.

"I don't like any of them," Sofian replied.

"Sofian," she said gently. "You are thirty years of age. You should be married by now."

Sofian sighed. Had he been just a prince and not the crown prince, there would not be this much pressure for him to find a bride.

"Let's talk about something else for now," Sofian said.

His mother sighed heavily. "Okay," she agreed.

***

Sofian heard the doors slide open. He frowned. Who would dare come into his room in the middle of the night? He heard footsteps approaching the bed. He jerked his head up. Morgan stood next to the bed with her hands on her hips. She was wearing a black silk nightgown.

"What is the meaning of this audacity?" he asked her.

"I can't sleep," she said.

"Okay?" He did not know what he was supposed to do about it. He did find it a little entertaining. Morgan was full of surprises.

"I couldn't sleep, and when you can't sleep you start thinking about things."

"And what were you thinking about?"

"You."

"Really?" Sofian sat up. Things were getting rather intriguing.

"Yes. You just kissed me and act like nothing happened," she complained. Sofian smiled. A glimpse of the moonlight shone into the room. It complemented her hazelnut skin color. Her beautiful curly hair was tied up into a messy ponytail. Morgan looked so attractive and she did not even know.

"How did you want me to act?" he asked.

"I don't know," she spat out.

"Kiss you again?"

"Yes, no. I am just saying be consistent."

Sofian took her hand and pulled her closer to him. "Tell me what you want me to do," he said.

"I said be consistent. Either stay normal or acknowledge the fact that we kissed," said Morgan.

Sofian leaned forward and put his arm around her waist. He pulled her closer to him. He put his head on her belly and just embraced her. "What are you doing?" she asked.

"I just want to hold you," he said to her and held her tightly. Morgan gasped. She placed one hand on his shoulder and rubbed the back of his head with the other hand. "Stay," he said to her.

"What?"

"Stay here."

"No, I am going to my own bed." Morgan tried to get out of Sofian's embrace, but he picked her up and put her on the bed instead. She screamed loudly and giggled. "Put me down!" she protested.

"Now you're in my bed. You might as well stay there." Sofian grinned at her.

Morgan growled at him. "And you say I am the weird one." Morgan lay on the bed and slammed her head into the pillow.

"You definitely are." Sofian lay down behind her and just wrapped his arm around her waist.

"I guess you want to hold me again," she said sarcastically.

"Yes. I am being consistent," he returned the sarcasm. He placed a small kiss on the back of her neck. It felt nice to have her in his arms.

"Well, don't get any funny ideas. I am only going to sleep here."

"What kind of ideas?"

"Nothing, goodnight."

Sofian smiled and released her from his embrace. She was right. He did not smile or laugh a lot. However he found himself smiling and laughing a lot in her presence. Even though they lay in silence, it was just nice to have her there.

The next morning, Sofian woke up to find Morgan sleeping on her back facing up. Her limbs were in opposite directions. He smiled to himself. She looked so adorable. He got out of bed and went to the bathroom. He washed his face and brushed his teeth. He had to have fresh breath and look good when she woke up. He could not have her see him looking a mess.

Sofian walked to the living room and asked the maids to bring breakfast to his bedroom. He returned to the bedroom and climbed back into bed. He just sat there and watched Morgan sleeping. He knew it was creepy but he could not help himself.

Morgan slowly opened her eyes. She stretched and made that weird noise again; the one she had made the last time she stretched in his presence. "Did you have good dreams?" he asked her.

"I did not dream of anything," she replied. She rolled to her side and just looked at him.

"You were talking in your sleep."

Morgan covered her face with her hands. "What did I say?" she asked.

"My name."

Morgan uncovered her face. "No, I did not," she said passionately.

Sofian raised his eyebrows. "You did." He dipped his head and pressed a small kiss against her soft lips. They were so inviting. Of course he accepted the invitation. He caressed her face with the back of his hand and kissed her again. She let out a sigh.

"Did you wake up early to brush your teeth before I woke up?" Morgan asked him.

"What?"

"Your breath is minty."

"I brushed."

"Were you scared I'd judge your morning breath?" she teased. She laughed a little. She had such a cute laugh and she looked beautiful when she laughed.

"Why would I?" Sofian had gotten caught. Fortunately there was knock on the door to disturb the current topic. "Come in," he said. The maids brought in two trays with breakfast for the two of them.

Chapter 17

Morgan had breakfast with Sofian in his bed. She felt so relaxed and so happy. She had slept well in his bed once again. She had dreamed of him and she had gotten caught. She had said his name in her sleep and he had heard her. So embarrassing.

She and Sofian talked as they ate. They had never done that before. Eaten in bed together. And yet it felt so normal. So real and so right. She was in no rush to get out of his bed, especially with it being a Saturday.

When they were finished eating, the maids came to get the trays. One of them informed the sheikh that there was someone waiting to see him. Sofian was reluctant to leave the bed.

"Did he give a name?" Sofian asked lazily.

"He said his name is Badir," the maid said to him. Sofian sprang out of bed as soon as he heard the name. Morgan wondered what was happening as she watched Sofian rush out of the room. She thought of eavesdropping but his quarters were large. She would not be able to hear. She could not go with him either because she was in her nightie.

Morgan walked out onto the balcony. The warm sun caressed her face. She smiled as the cool, subtle breeze brushed through her hair. She felt as though she was in some kind of dream. She had never experienced such luxury. She heard Sofian walking back into the room.

"That was quick," she said as she walked back into the room. She gasped and quickly turned away from Sofian. He was in nothing but his boxers. "Why are you naked?" she asked.

"I am getting dressed," he replied. "Why are you acting all shy? Have you not seen an undressed man before?"

She hadn't, well not in real life. She did not make a habit of sleeping in other men's beds either. And yet she had slept in Sofian's bed twice.

"It's just not appropriate," she said, deflecting the question.

"I have an important matter to attend to," he said to her. Morgan turned to look at him. She was relieved to find him fully clothed.

"Do you need me to come?" Morgan asked.

He shook his head. He turned on his heel and rushed out of the room. Morgan was curious as to what was going on. There definitely was something. First it was the text and then him rushing to speak to this Badir person. Since they had come back to Kaslan, Morgan had gone almost everywhere with Sofian, even if it was not necessary. Now he was going without her.

Morgan headed back to her quarters. As she walked through the hallway and into the living room and until she was out of Sofian's quarters, the maids stared at her. Some of them whispered among each other. Morgan just shook her head and ignored them.

***

Sofian walked back to his quarters feeling dejected. He was coming from a prison. Badir had successfully caught his brother's killers and anyone associated with them. However it did not comfort him. Samir was still dead. He thought some of his anger and resentment would disappear after he had arrested the Khans but that was not the case.

He had gone to the prison, and he had faced his brother's killers. He felt so much anger flow through him. He wanted to rip their heads off with his bare hands. He so badly wanted them to pay for their sin with their lives. However Sofian knew that killing them was not the answer, and it was unlike him. He was not a killer.

Instead of walking into his quarters, he found himself walking into Morgan's quarters. She was sitting on the sofa with her phone in her hand. Sofian went to sit down next to her and just wrapped his arms around her.

"Sofian, what's going on?" Morgan asked. He just rested his head on her shoulder and held her tightly.

"I saw my brother's murderers," he said to her.

"Huh?"

Sofian released her from his embrace. Morgan turned to face him. "The man who came to see me this morning, Badir, he arrested the men that killed my brother," he said to her.

Morgan's brown eyes widened. "Oh." She reached out and rubbed his arms.

"I wanted to kill them."

"That's understandable."

"I thought I would have at least have some peace after seeing them behind bars."

"That is also understandable." She stroked his face. "It takes time. Allow yourself to grieve." Morgan pulled him into her arms. She held him so tightly and just rubbed his back. Sofian welcomed her comfort.

He pulled out of her embrace and kissed her. He took his time, slowly and gently kissing her. He explored her mouth as if it was an undiscovered land. Morgan wrapped her arms around his neck and kissed him back.

"I'm being consistent," he whispered to her.

"No, you're being sarcastic," she corrected him.

He smiled and kissed her again. Her lips were so soft. She felt good. He liked how her body felt against his body. Her chest was pressed against his. Her scent filled up the room. She smelled good. He wondered why it took so long to realize just how much he wanted her. Morgan was everything he wanted and needed. She was intelligent, funny, beautiful, and she had a good heart. He loved her thick curly hair. He loved the fact she talked in her sleep. It was so adorable. She was adorable, and feisty and random. He had never met a woman like her. Morgan was the best thing that had ever happened to him.

Chapter 18

Morgan returned to Kaslan just in time for the king's birthday celebration. She had gone back to the States for a couple of meetings. Sofian had been too busy preparing to be the crown prince. So he could not go. Morgan had only returned home for four days. In those four days she had gone to meet with Jackie's Pharmacies. She had also gone to the office to check on the current projects.

It had felt odd to be back in the States. It was weird not seeing Sofian for four days. It was not normal. Four days had been too long. The only good thing was that she had gotten to see Brooke. She had disliked not being able to see her best friend for so long. It was nice to finally see her again and talk with her.

As soon as Morgan arrived back in Kaslan, she went to her quarters to get ready for the party. The king had personally invited her and therefore she could not miss it. She got into the shower and quickly bathed. That walk-in shower had been one of the best things about living in the palace. It was much bigger than her own shower in America and it was just nicer.

When she had finished showering she towel dried herself and applied apricot lotion on her skin. She slipped on an ankle-length royal blue dress with a boat neck and a lace back. She straightened her hair. She styled it into a low bun, and parted her hair at the side. She left her fringe fall to the right side of her face. She applied burgundy lipstick and finally slipped into her black shoes.

Morgan walked into the palace courtyard where the king's birthday celebration was being held. As she walked outside, she immediately saw Sofian. He was standing with Zara. He was dressed in a black tuxedo and a black bow tie. His hair was neatly cut in a short back and sides style as always. His rough beard was just a few days old. It added an edge to his look.

Sofian looked gorgeous. Morgan wanted to run into his arms and just kiss him. She had not seen him for four long days and so badly wanted to embrace him but she knew that she could not do that. She walked over to him and bowed her head when she approached him. For a moment he did not say anything. He just stared at her.

"You're back," Sofian said to her.

"I am back," Morgan replied. Sofian did not say anything else. He just stared at her. She too stared at him and said nothing. Just being there close to him made her heart race. She felt her stomach knot up. Zara cleared her throat. Sofian and Morgan turned to look at her.

"Have the pair of you forgotten that I am here?" Zara said to them.

"What do you mean by that?" Sofian asked her.

"The way you are glaring into each other's eyes. She still has not even greeted me yet."

Morgan gasped. She turned sharply and looked at Zara. "I apologize, your highness," she said and bowed her head.

Zara dismissed her bow with her hand. "I am just teasing you," she said with a smile. Zara was a little taller and slimmer than Morgan. She had beautiful almond-colored skin and long jet-black hair. She had a long neck and high cheekbones. She was very beautiful and elegant.

"Have you been well?" Morgan asked Zara.

"I have, thank you."

There were so many guests at the party. Morgan had never been to an Arabic party or a royal one. In the past month, she had experienced so much Arabic tradition. She was enjoying herself and wanted to experience more.

The king called for everyone's attention. "Thank you all for attending my sixty-fifth birthday," he said. The guests all cheered. Morgan was shocked that he was sixty-five. He looked ten years younger than that. The king then announced his abdication. He officially made everyone aware that he was stepping down from the throne and that Sofian was going to take his place.

Sofian was to have his coronation in a month's time. After his coronation, then he would officially be king. Morgan felt a range of mixed emotions. She had been with Sofian through this crash course to be king. He had to learn so much and attend so many meetings. She knew that he was fit for the position. He was going to make a fine king. She was happy for him.

The sad thing was that she was going to have to pack up and return home. How long was she going to be Sofian's assistant with kissing benefits? She could not even just date him like normal people date. He was a prince. People talked. It would become public knowledge and then all the criticism would start. But how she was going to live without him? Four days without him had felt like four decades.

Morgan snapped out of her thoughts when she heard everyone cheering. The women were ululating. She smiled. The atmosphere made her both happy and sad.

"Let's go dance," Zara said to Morgan.

"What? Oh no. I don't dance," she said. Zara smiled and took Morgan's hand.

"Everyone dances."

Morgan laughed and followed Zara. They went to join the others dancing in the courtyard. Zara showed Morgan how to belly dance. Morgan was not a very good dancer but she tried. Some of the women circled her and started ululating. Morgan wanted to stop dancing but Zara encouraged her to keep dancing.

At the end of the night, Morgan felt so exhausted and just wanted to sleep. She had enjoyed herself but was happy to retire to her chambers. She kicked her shoes off and threw herself on the sofa.

"Tired?" Sofian said as he walked into the room.

"I am," Morgan replied as she sat up. Sofian knelt in front of Morgan and took her feet into his hands.

"Of course you are tired. You've been very busy tonight." He started rubbing her feet. Just what Morgan needed. However it surprised her. She had the future king of Kaslan on his knees rubbing her feet.

"You're massaging my feet?"

"I'm massaging your feet."

Morgan took a deep breath. "I have to go back home," she said.

"Why?" Sofian looked up.

"I have no place here, Sofian." She reached out and touched his shoulder. "You will be king soon. I can't be in your way."

"You won't be in my way. You will be at my side."

"My work here is done," she said, as much as it hurt her to say.

"I am not asking you to stay as my assistant." Sofian stopped rubbing her feet. He grabbed her thighs and pulled her closer to him. Morgan gasped.

"Hey!"

"I am asking you to stay by my side, as my wife."

Morgan burst into laughter. "What?" Maybe she had not heard him correctly. Sofian reached into his pocket and fished out a black velvet box. "Wait!" Morgan shouted before he opened it.

"What?" Sofian asked her.

"Are you sure you want to open that box and ask me that question? Because once you do that, you can't take it back."

Sofian smiled. "I'm sure." He opened the box and revealed a diamond ring. "I loved you longer than I knew I did. These past four days were so dull without you. I was able to get through Samir's death because of you and I was able to be the crown prince with your help and advice. I can't be without you. I don't want to be without you," he said.

Morgan moved closer to Sofian and pressed a small kiss against his lips. "I'll marry you," she said and kissed him again. No man had ever made her feel the way Sofian had. His presence had affected her from the first moment she had spoken to him. The more time she had spent with him, the more she had grown to love and respect him. Of course she would marry him.

"You will?" Sofian sounded so shocked. Morgan laughed and nodded. Her eyes welled up. "Good because I'd die if you said no."

"I love you too much to say no." Morgan kissed his cheeks and his lips. Sofian slipped the ring on her finger. He touched her face and caressed her cheek with his thumb. He searched her eyes before he kissed her.

Epilogue

After Morgan had agreed to marry Sofian, she had to prepare to be the crown princess. She had to learn Arabic language, learn about the Kaslan culture, she had to do so many things she had never had to do in her life. Fortunately for her, his parents had accepted her to be their daughter-in-law. Morgan had been so worried that her not being from an upper-class background would hinder her relationship with Sofian but it had not.

She had done some charity work and had gone to many events. The public had taken a liking into her. She spoke her mind, she was free-spirited and she was down-to-earth. They felt that Morgan was someone they could relate to.

Brooke had been so happy to hear about Morgan and Sofian getting married. She felt the need to gloat about being correct. She had predicted that the two would fall in love. She was also excited about going to Kaslan for the wedding and being a bridesmaid.

The coronation had been a bore. Both Sofian and Morgan had been bored at the ceremony. It was so formal. So many ministers, governors and other royal family members had attended the coronation. Sofian had flown Morgan's family to Kaslan for the coronation.

Then there was the wedding. It took place a month after the coronation. Morgan had wanted a simple wedding but being the crown princess did not give her that option. The wedding had been so extravagant and elaborate. So many people attended. So much money had been spent on it. Her dress alone had costed over fifty thousand dollars.

"I'm glad I married you," Sofian whispered to Morgan as they danced in the middle of the room.

"I'm glad you did," Morgan replied. All eyes were on them as they danced. The guests cheered and clapped. There were others ululating. Sofian dipped his head and kissed his wife.

"All those times you stared at me with an expressionless gaze, what were you thinking?" Morgan asked Sofian. She had always wanted to ask him about it.

"Different things," he replied.

"Like?"

"I was either taking in your beauty or I was just wanting to take you."

Morgan's eyes flew open. She pushed him playfully. "You possessed such dirty thoughts," she said.

"I am a man." Sofian shrugged his shoulders.

"All those times?" Morgan shook her head. There were too many times it had happened.

"In fact I want to take you now."

"Sofian! There are people around."

"So what? I desire my wife. Is there anything wrong with that?"

"No." Morgan giggled. Sofian pressed a kiss against her cheek and then her neck. She giggled even more.

"Then let's go start our wedding night early, Queen Morgan Bukhari."

"You're so cheesy." Morgan burst into laughter. Sofian took her hand.

"Thank you, everyone, for coming. I hope you can continue to enjoy the reception. My wife and I are now leaving," Sofian announced to everyone. It was better to just announce their departure. The crowd cheered and clapped as they left. Brooke whistled really loudly. Morgan smiled and shook her head. She expected no less from Brooke.

"Let's go, my sheikh," Morgan said to Sofian as they walked out of their wedding reception.

What to read next?

If you liked this book, you will also like *The Weekend Girlfriend*. Another interesting book is *Two Reasons to Be Single*.

The Weekend Girlfriend

Jessica has worked hard to be the paralegal that hotshot, sexy attorney Kyle needs. Unfortunately he doesn't see her as just his paralegal but also his own personal assistant. When he blames her for a mix-up in his personal life, Jessica sees no other option but to quit, thinking that her time with him is over. Much to her surprise, Kyle makes a proposition to her that she never thought she would hear coming from his lips. He needs a temporary girlfriend for his sister's wedding and he wants her to be that person. Jessica accepts the challenge and finds herself thrown into his world, learning things about him she never knew. The more time she spends with him outside of work, the more she is drawn to Kyle. As the wedding draws near, she finds herself fighting off some strong feelings for the man. When the wedding weekend is over, will Jessica be able to walk away from Kyle with her heart intact?

Two Reasons to Be Single

Olivia Parker has a job doing what she loves, a wonderful family and plenty of friends, but no luck in the love department. Tired of worrying about it, she decides to swear off love completely and focus on all the good things in her life. Just as she makes her firm resolution, Jake Harper arrives in town and knocks her plans into a tailspin. As the excited single ladies of Morning Glory surround the extremely attractive newcomer, Olivia steers clear of the "casserole brigade," as she calls the women, and tries to keep her distance from Jake. Instead, a variety of situations throw them together and they get to know each other better. They both have reasons for not wanting to get involved in a relationship, but the chemistry between them ignites, even as they desperately attempt to keep it at bay. As things heat up between Olivia and Jake, there is an aura of mystery about him that leaves Olivia certain that he is hiding something. When Jake disappears for a few days without telling Olivia that he is going out of town, she hates the way it makes her feel, and it reminds her of why she was giving up on dating in the first place. As Olivia's feelings for Jake grow, so does the need to find out what exactly brought him to Morning Glory and what he's been hiding.

About Emily Walters

Emily Walters lives in California with her beloved husband, three daughters, and two dogs. She began writing after high school, but it took her ten long years of writing for newspapers and magazines until she realized that fiction is her real passion. Emily likes to create a mental movie in her reader's mind about charismatic characters, their passionate relationships and interesting adventures. When she isn't writing romantic stories, she can be found reading a fiction book, jogging, or traveling with her family. She loves Starbucks, Matt Damon and Argentinian tango.

One Last Thing…

If you believe that *The Sheikh's Assistant i*s worth sharing, would you spend a minute to let your friends know about it?

If this book lets them have a great time, they will be enormously grateful to you – as will I.

Emily

www.EmilyWaltersBooks.com